LA GRANGE
PUBLIC LIBRARY

10 West Cossitt Avenue
La Grange, IL 60525
lagrangelibrary.org 708.352.0576

DEMCO

Mighty Mighty MONSTERS

MONSTER

MANSION

STONE ARCH BOOKS

a capstone imprint

created by Sean O'Reilly
illustrated by Arcana Studio

Mighty Mighty Monsters are published by Stone Arch Books, A Capstone Imprint 151 Good Counsel Drive, P.O. Box 669 Mankato, Minnesota 56002 *www.capstonepub. com* Copyright © 2011 by Stone Arch Books All rights reserved. No part of this publication may be reproduced in whole or in part, or stored in a retrieval system, or transmitted in any form or by any means, electronic, mechanical, photocopying, recording, or otherwise, without written permission of the publisher.

Library of Congress Cataloging-in-Publication Data
O'Reilly, Sean, 1974-
  Monster mansion / written by Sean O'Reilly ; illustrated by Arcana Studio.
    p. cm. -- (Mighty Mighty Monsters)
  Summary: The Mighty Mighty Monsters are convinced that they can spend the night in a haunted mansion until they encounter the ghosts.
  ISBN 978-1-4342-2152-0 (library binding)
  1. Graphic novels. [1. Graphic novels. 2. Monsters--Fiction. 3. Ghosts--Fiction.] I.
Arcana Studio. II. Title.
  PZ7.7.O74Mon 2010
  741.5'973--dc22   2010004123)

Summary: When you're a Mighty Mighty Monster, spending the night in a haunted mansion should be easy. Unfortunately, no one told that to the ghosts.

Printed in the United States of America in Stevens Point, Wisconsin.
032010
005741WZF10

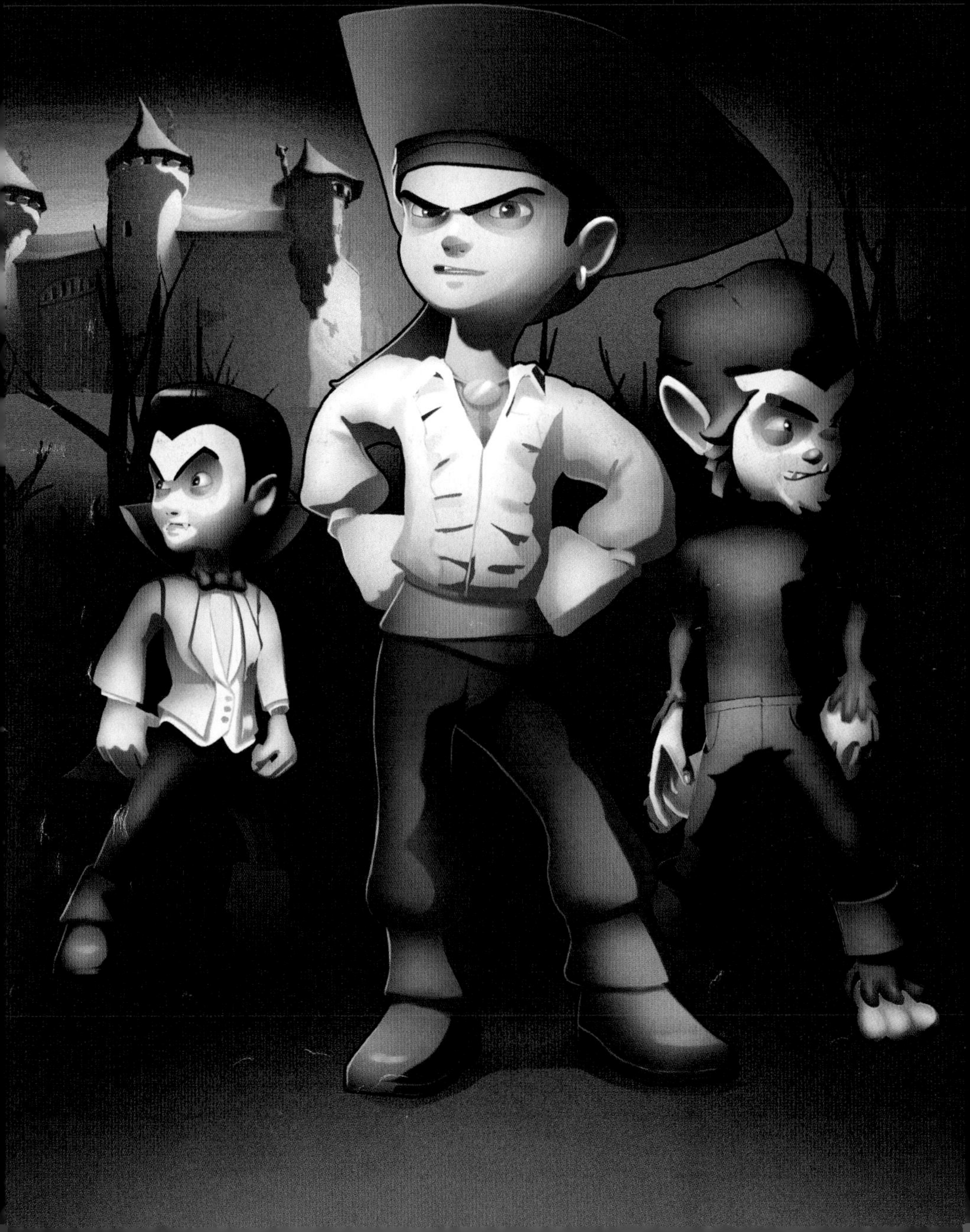

In a strange corner of the world known as Transylmania . . .

Legendary monsters were born.

WELCOME TO
TRANSYLMANIA

But long before their frightful fame, these classic creatures faced fears of their own.

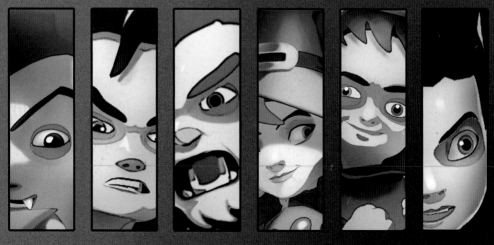

To take on terrifying teachers and homework horrors, they formed the most fearsome friendship on Earth . . .

Mighty Mighty MONSTERS

Vlad

Talbot

Witchita

Milton

Poto

Frankie

Igor

Mary

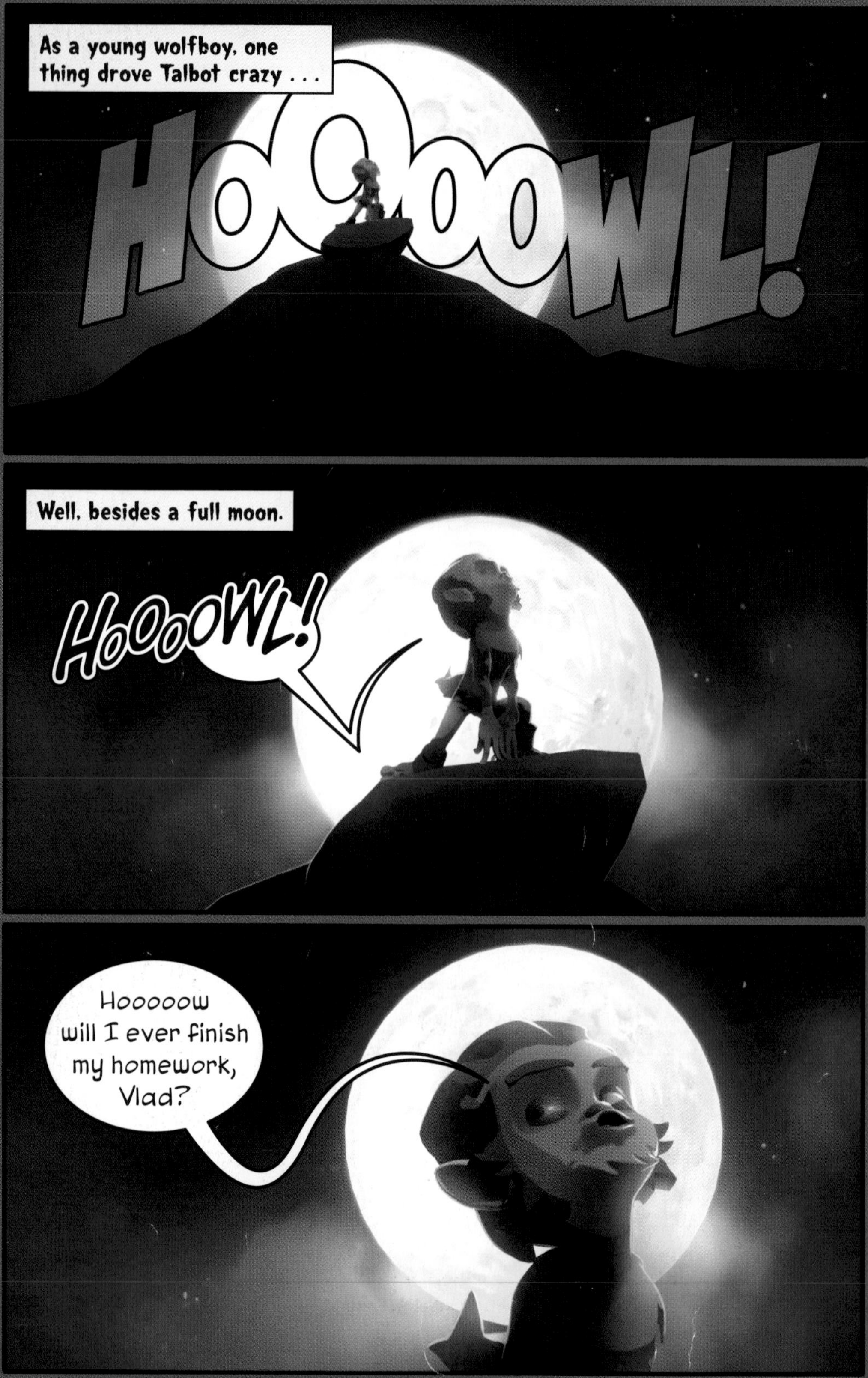
As a young wolfboy, one thing drove Talbot crazy . . .
HOOOOOWL!
Well, besides a full moon.
HOOOOWL!
Hoooooow will I ever finish my homework, Vlad?

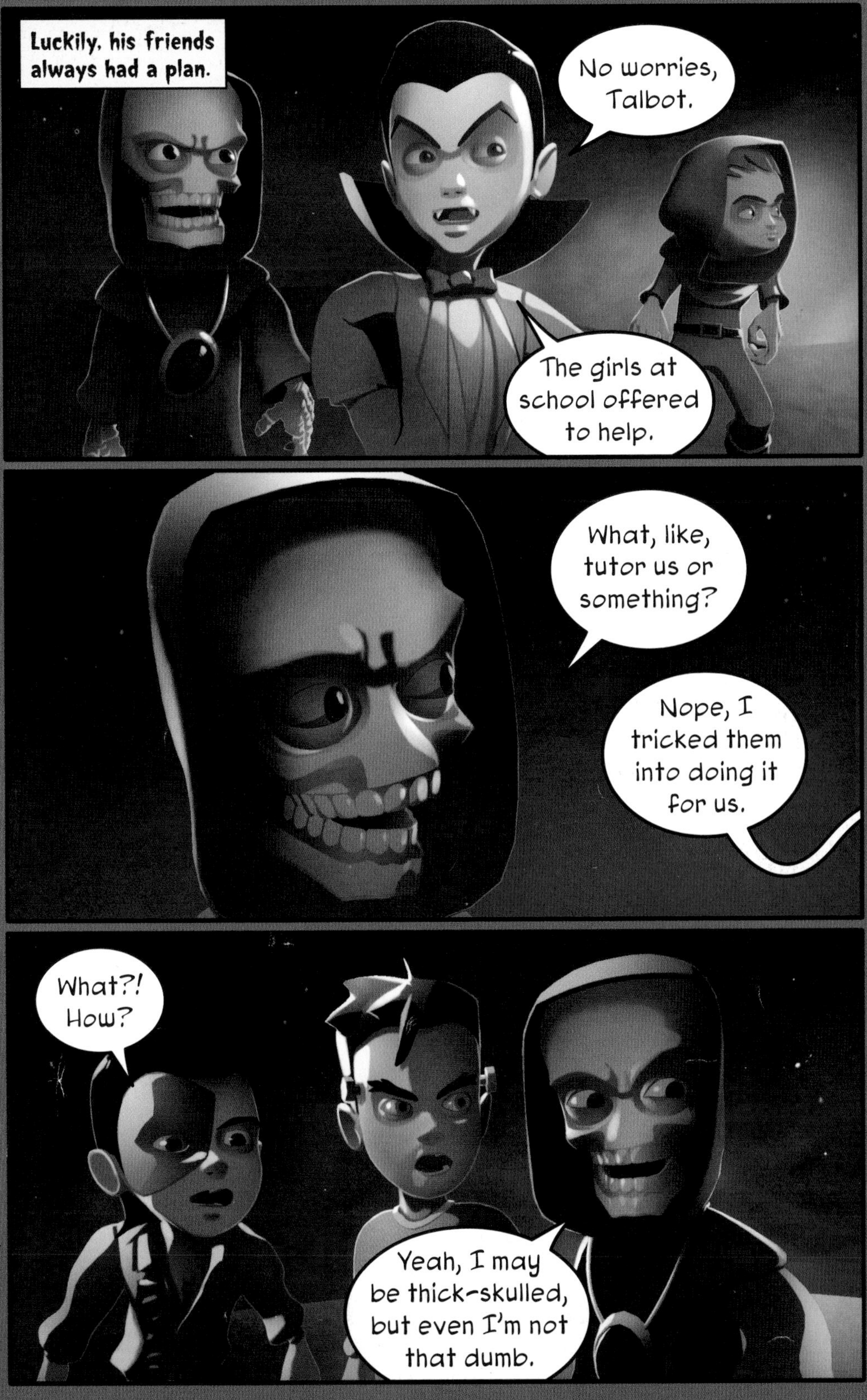
Luckily, his friends always had a plan.
No worries, Talbot.
The girls at school offered to help.
What, like, tutor us or something?
Nope, I tricked them into doing it for us.
What?! How?
Yeah, I may be thick-skulled, but even I'm not that dumb.

Well, they're not doing it for free.

I sort of made a bet with them.

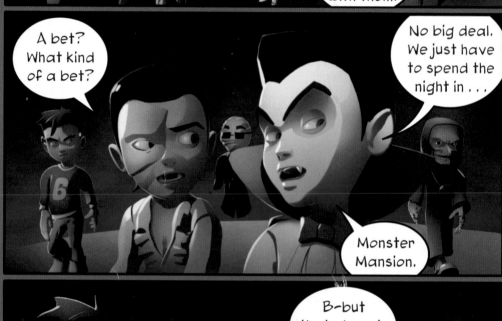

A bet? What kind of a bet?

No big deal. We just have to spend the night in . . .

Monster Mansion.

B-but that place is s-scary!

Have you looked in the mirror lately, Igor.

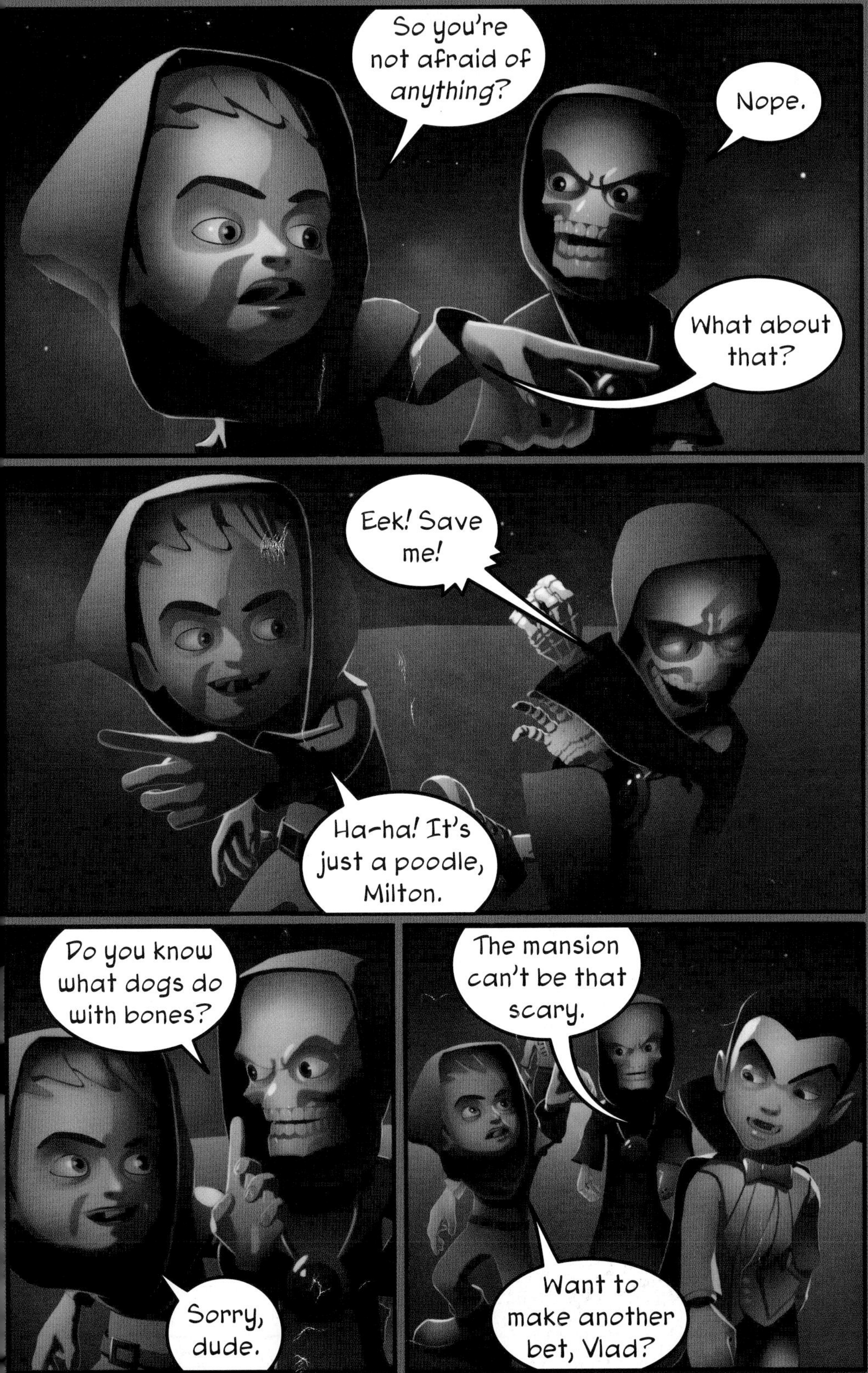
So you're not afraid of anything?
Nope.
What about that?
Eek! Save me!
Ha-ha! It's just a poodle, Milton.
Do you know what dogs do with bones?
Sorry, dude.
The mansion can't be that scary.
Want to make another bet, Vlad?

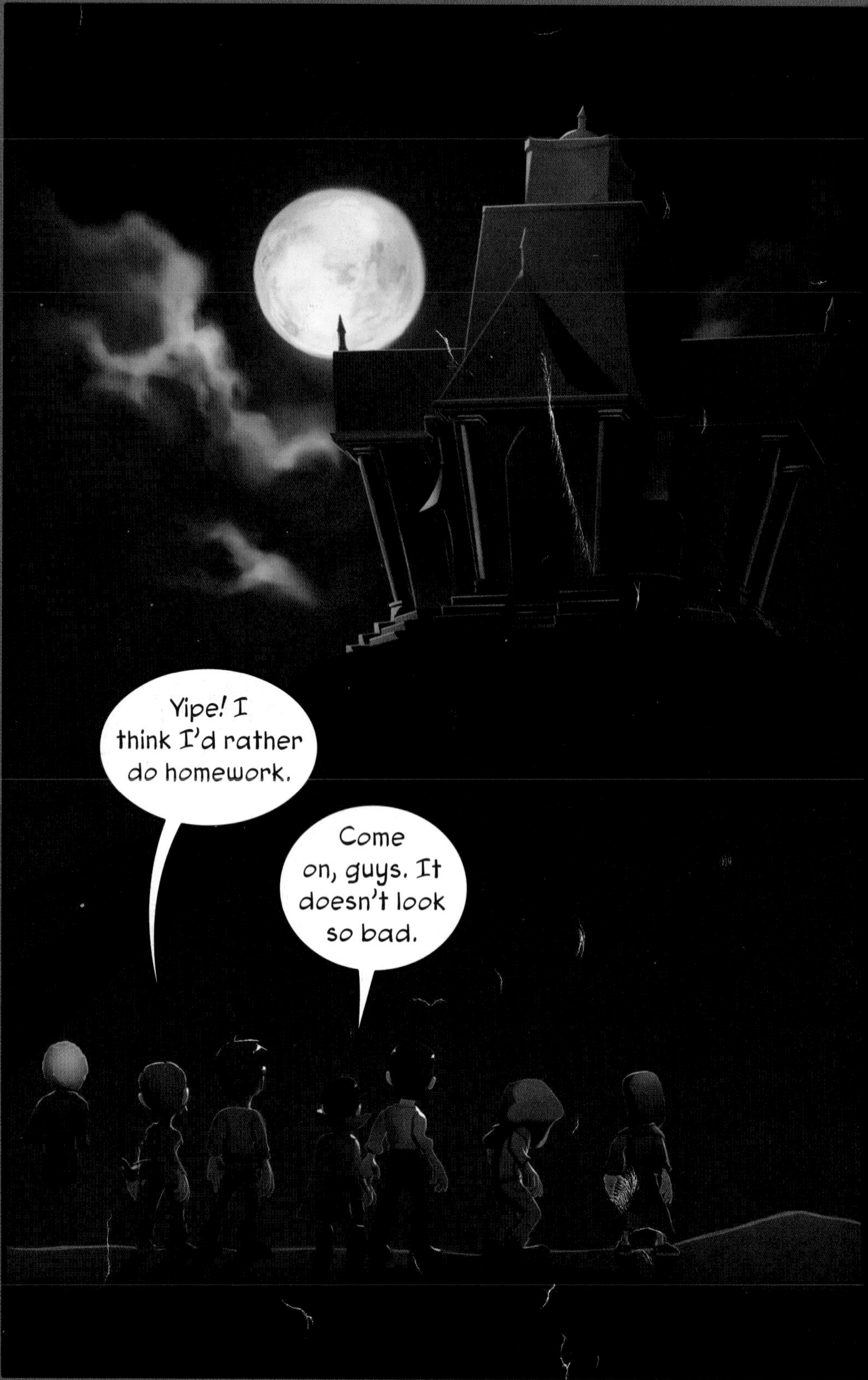
Yipe! I think I'd rather do homework.
Come on, guys. It doesn't look so bad.

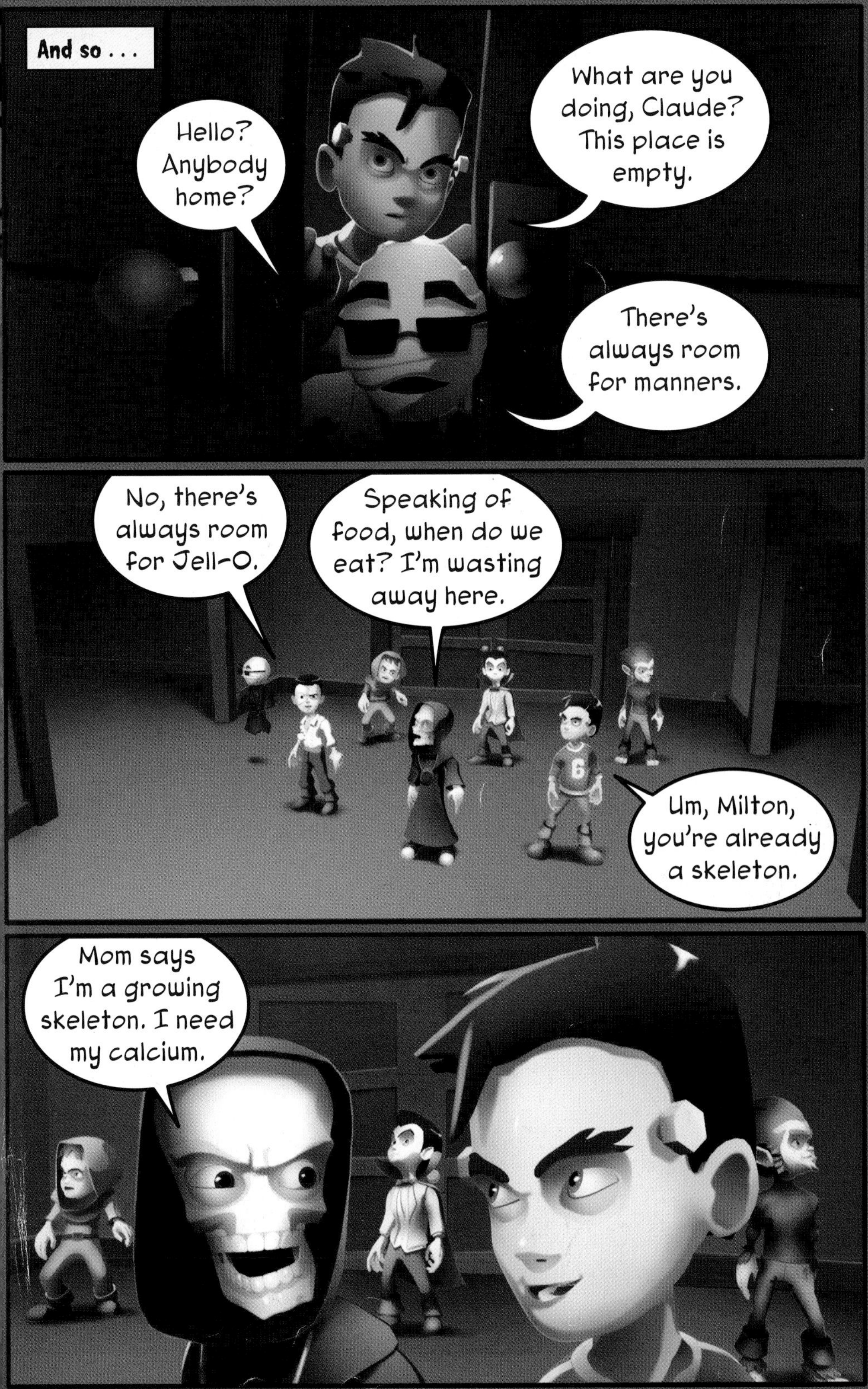
And so . . .
Hello? Anybody home?
What are you doing, Claude? This place is empty.
There's always room for manners.
No, there's always room for Jell-O.
Speaking of food, when do we eat? I'm wasting away here.
Um, Milton, you're already a skeleton.
Mom says I'm a growing skeleton. I need my calcium.

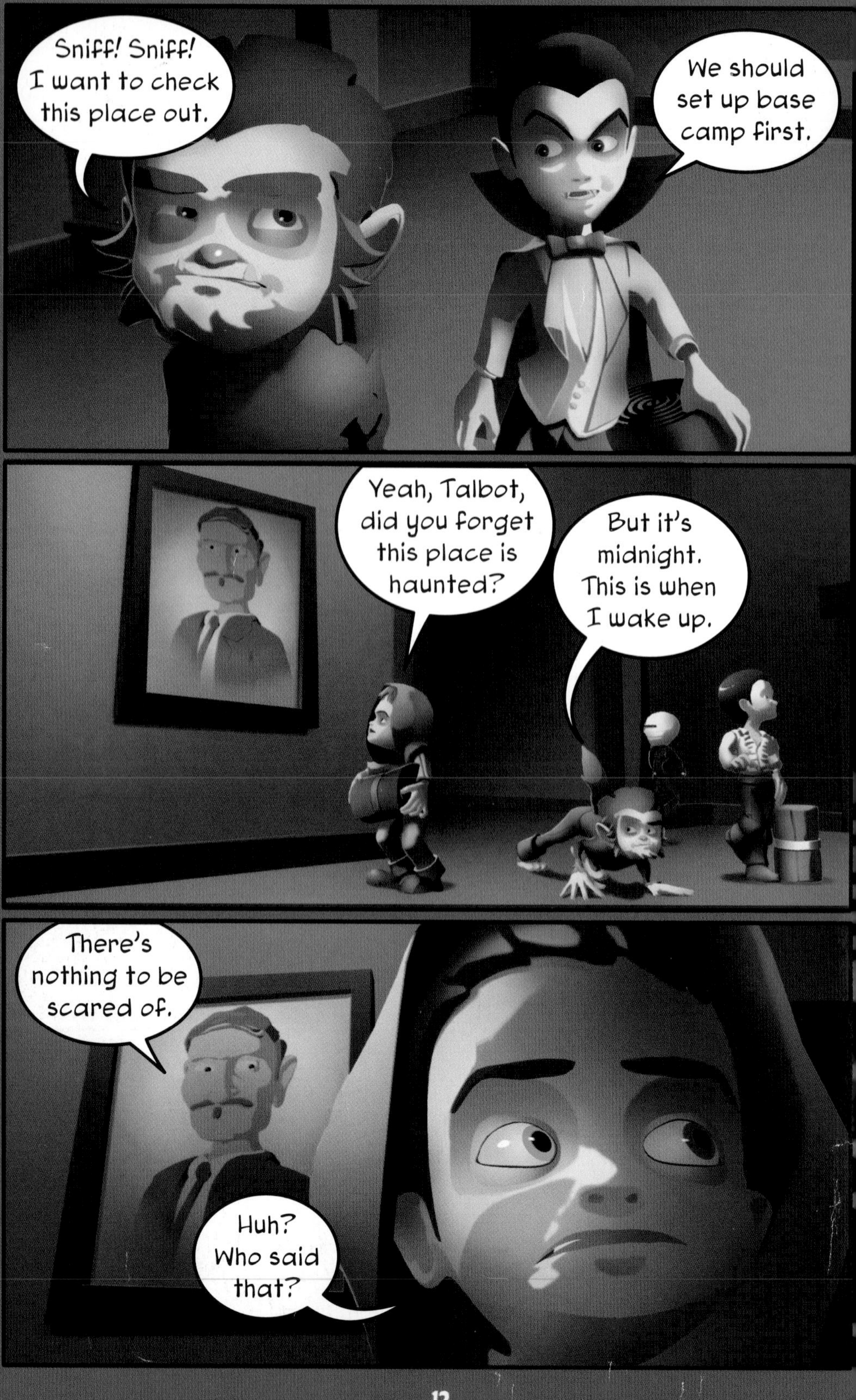
Sniff! Sniff! I want to check this place out.
We should set up base camp first.
Yeah, Talbot, did you forget this place is haunted?
But it's midnight. This is when I wake up.
There's nothing to be scared of.
Huh? Who said that?

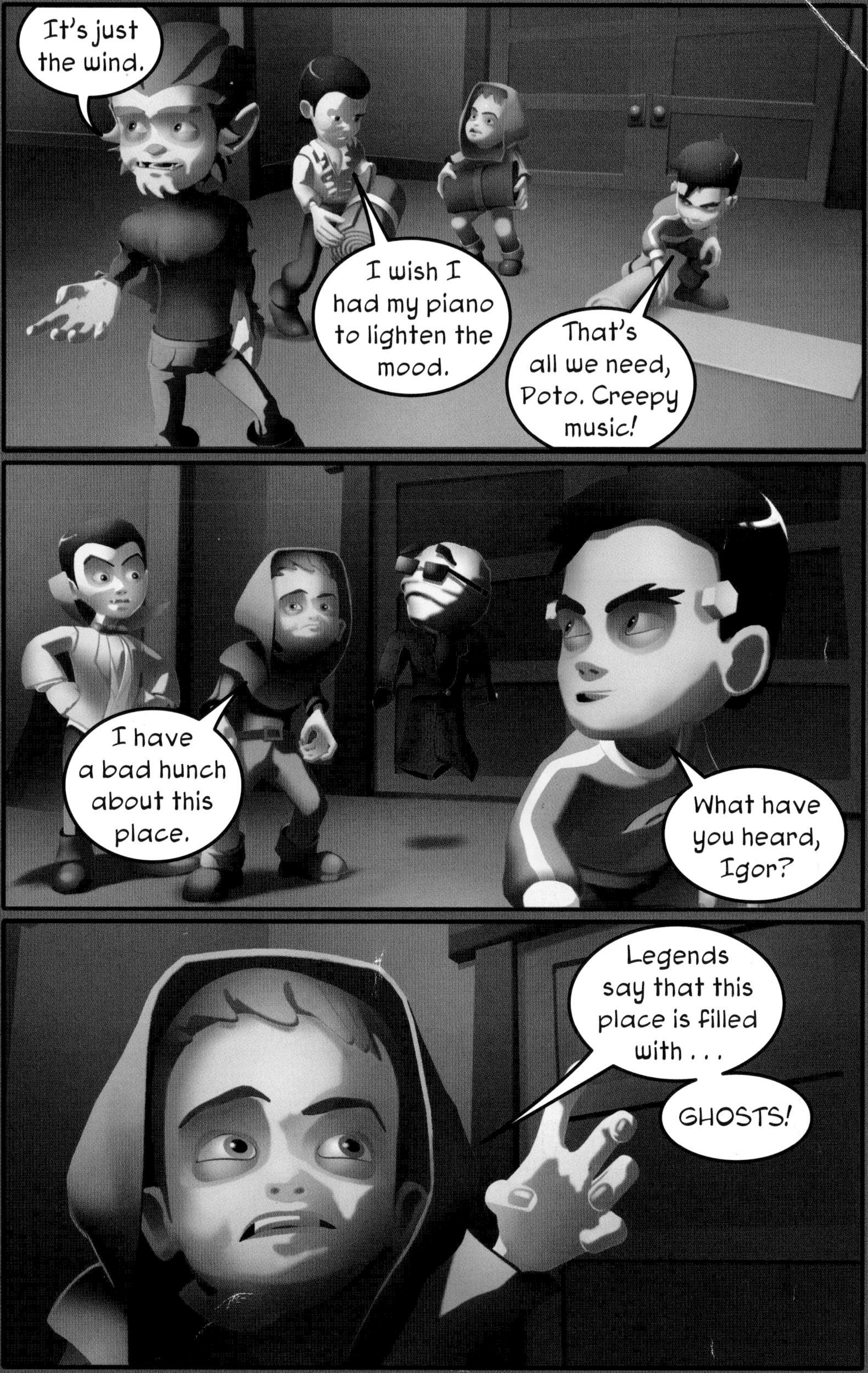
It's just the wind.
I wish I had my piano to lighten the mood.
That's all we need, Poto. Creepy music!
I have a bad hunch about this place.
What have you heard, Igor?
Legends say that this place is filled with . . .
GHOSTS!

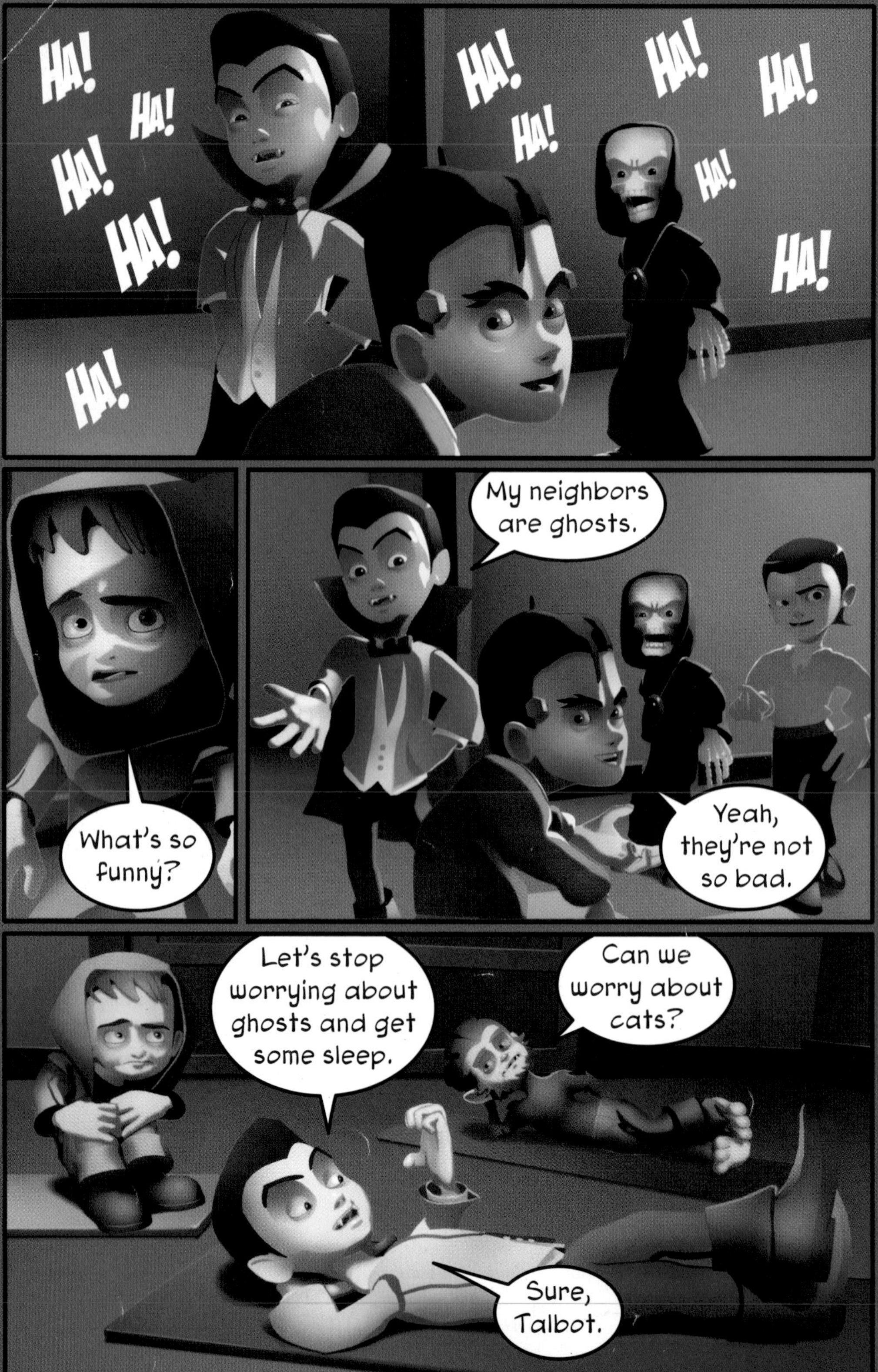
HA!
HA!
HA!
HA!
HA!
HA!
HA!
HA!
HA!
HA!
HA!
What's so funny?
My neighbors are ghosts.
Yeah, they're not so bad.
Let's stop worrying about ghosts and get some sleep.
Can we worry about cats?
Sure, Talbot.

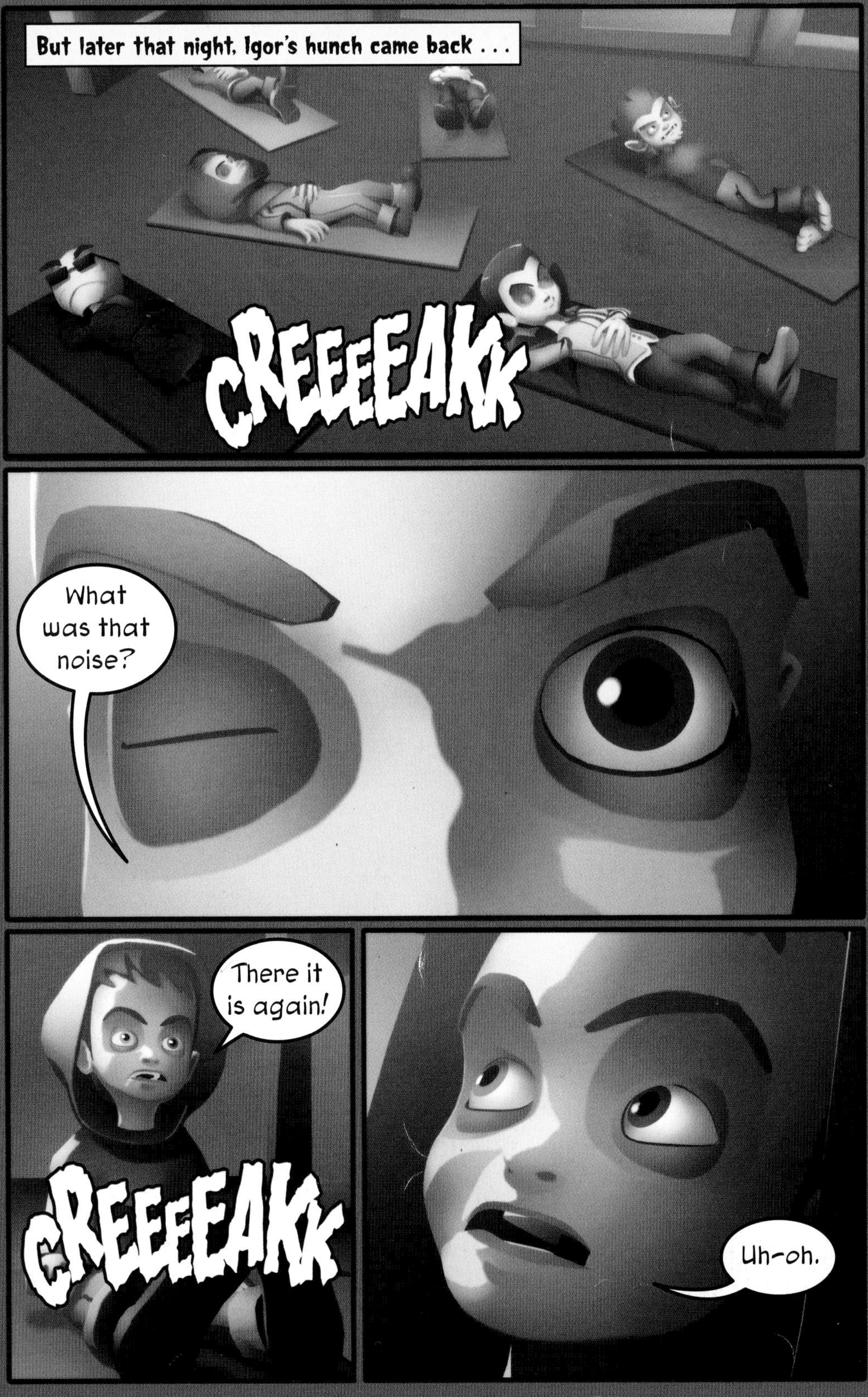
But later that night, Igor's hunch came back . . .
CREEEEAKK
What was that noise?
There it is again!
CREEEEAKK
Uh-oh.

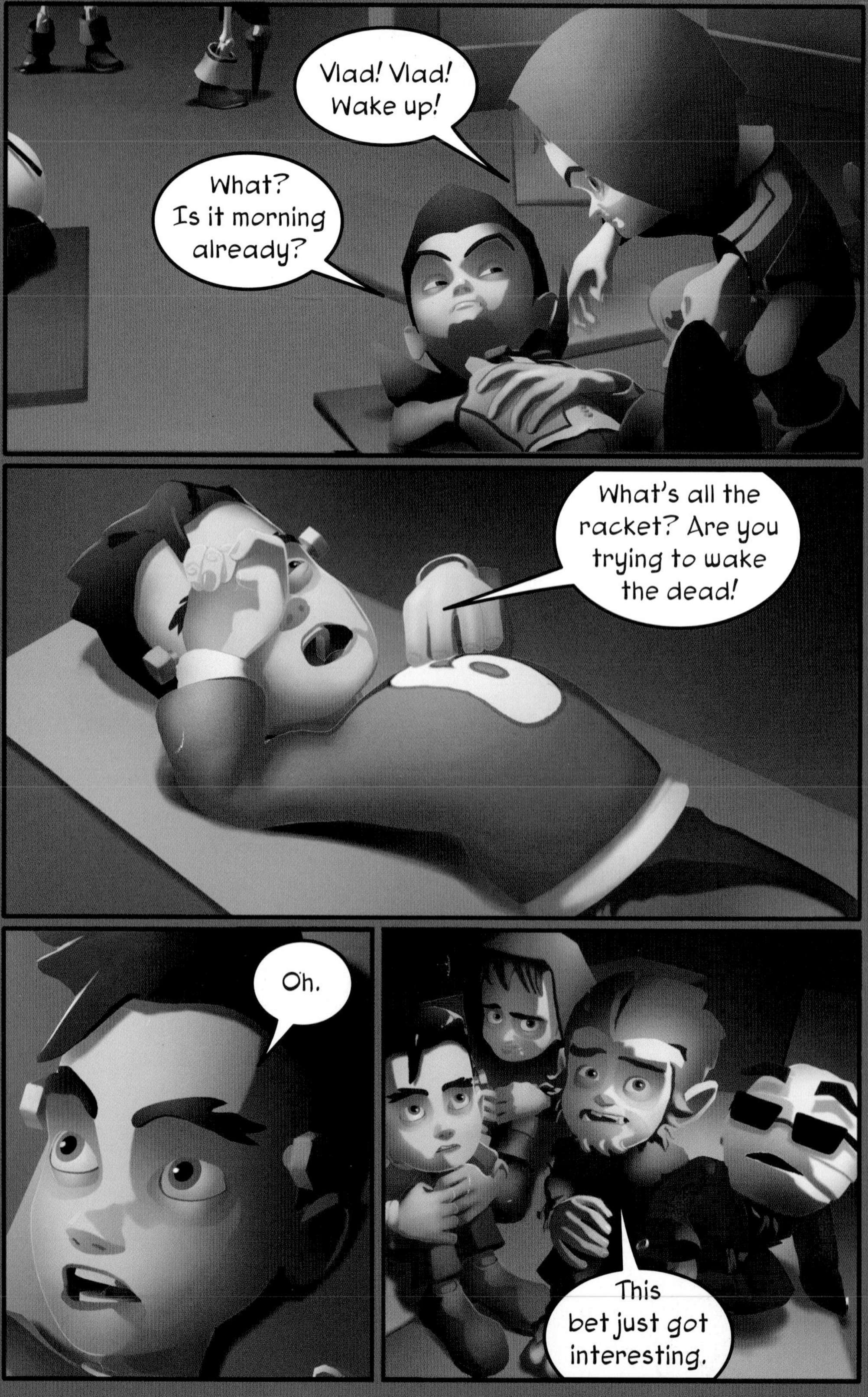
Vlad! Vlad! Wake up!
What? Is it morning already?
What's all the racket? Are you trying to wake the dead!
Oh.
This bet just got interesting.

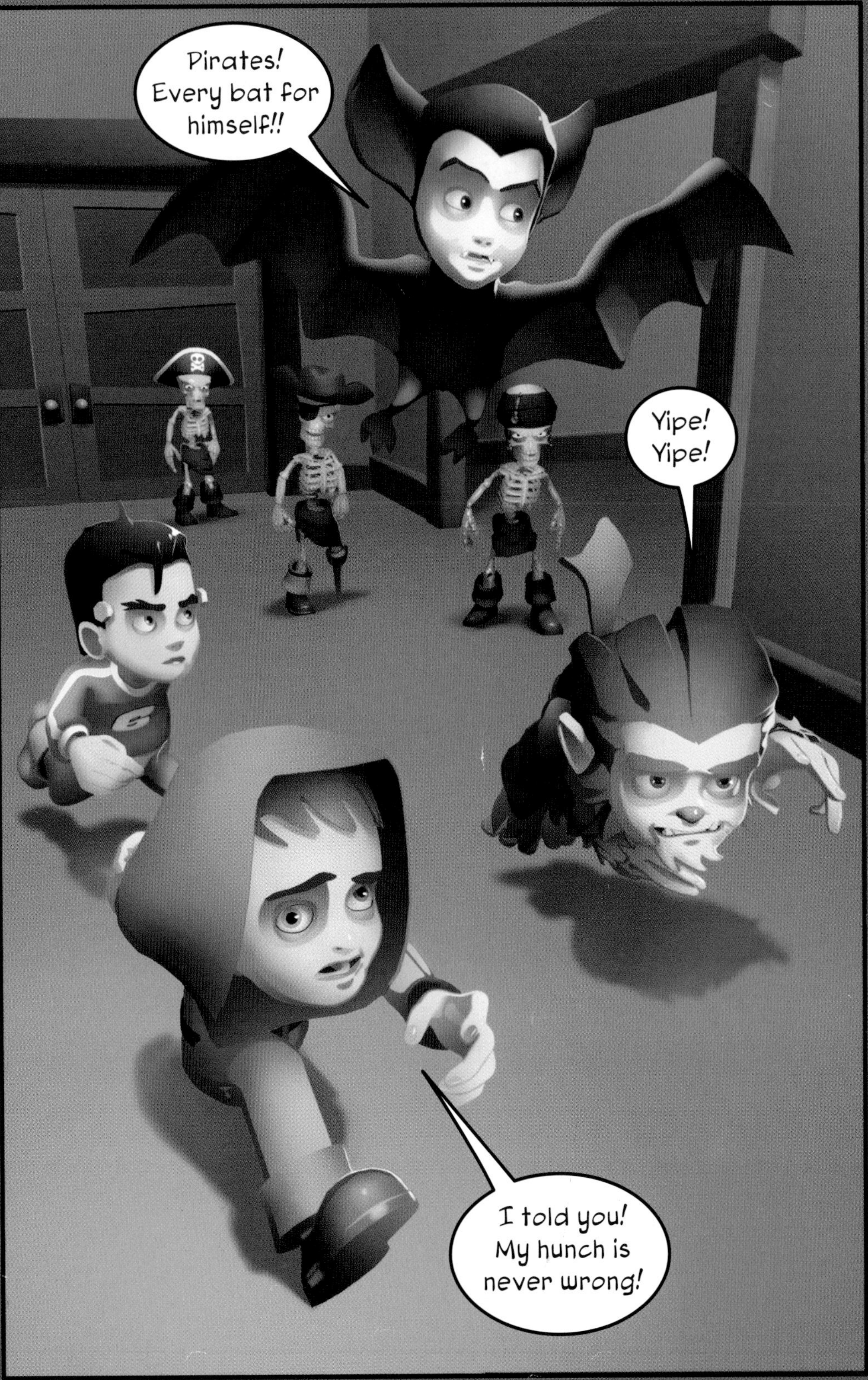
Pirates! Every bat for himself!!
Yipe! Yipe!
I told you! My hunch is never wrong!

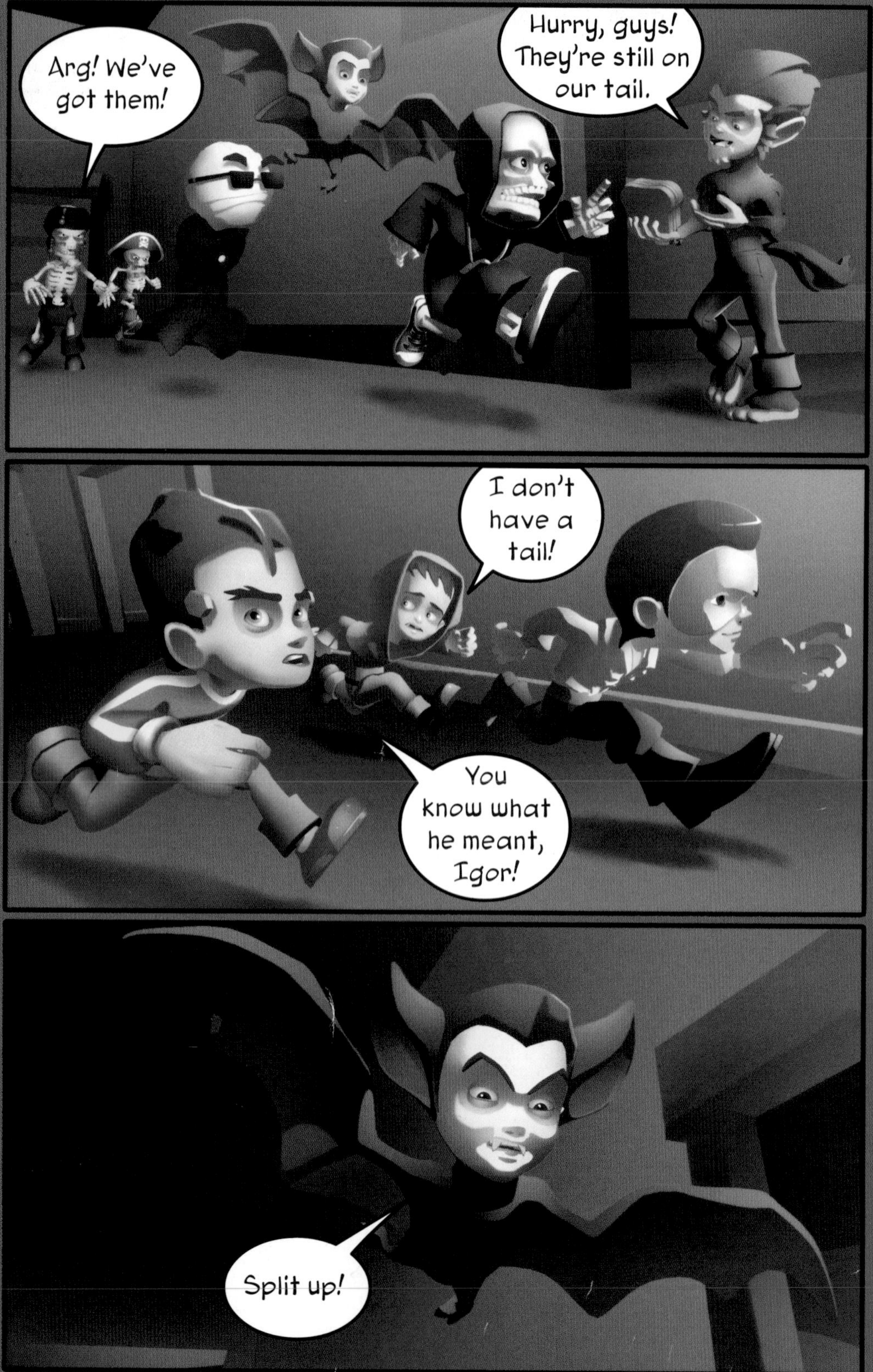
Arg! We've got them!
Hurry, guys! They're still on our tail.
I don't have a tail!
You know what he meant, Igor!
Split up!

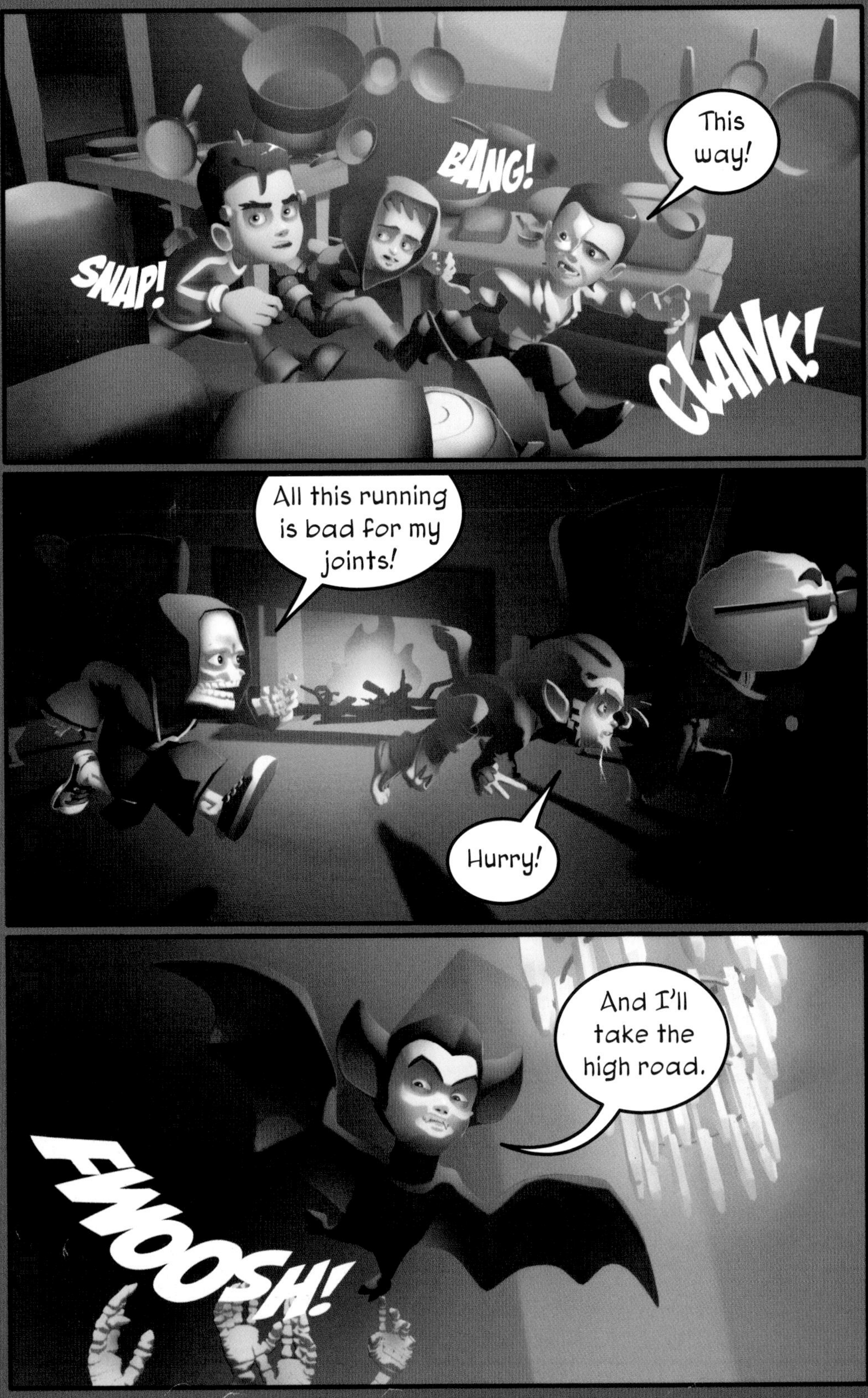
SNAP!
BANG!
This way!
CLANK!
All this running is bad for my joints!
Hurry!
And I'll take the high road.
FWOOSH!

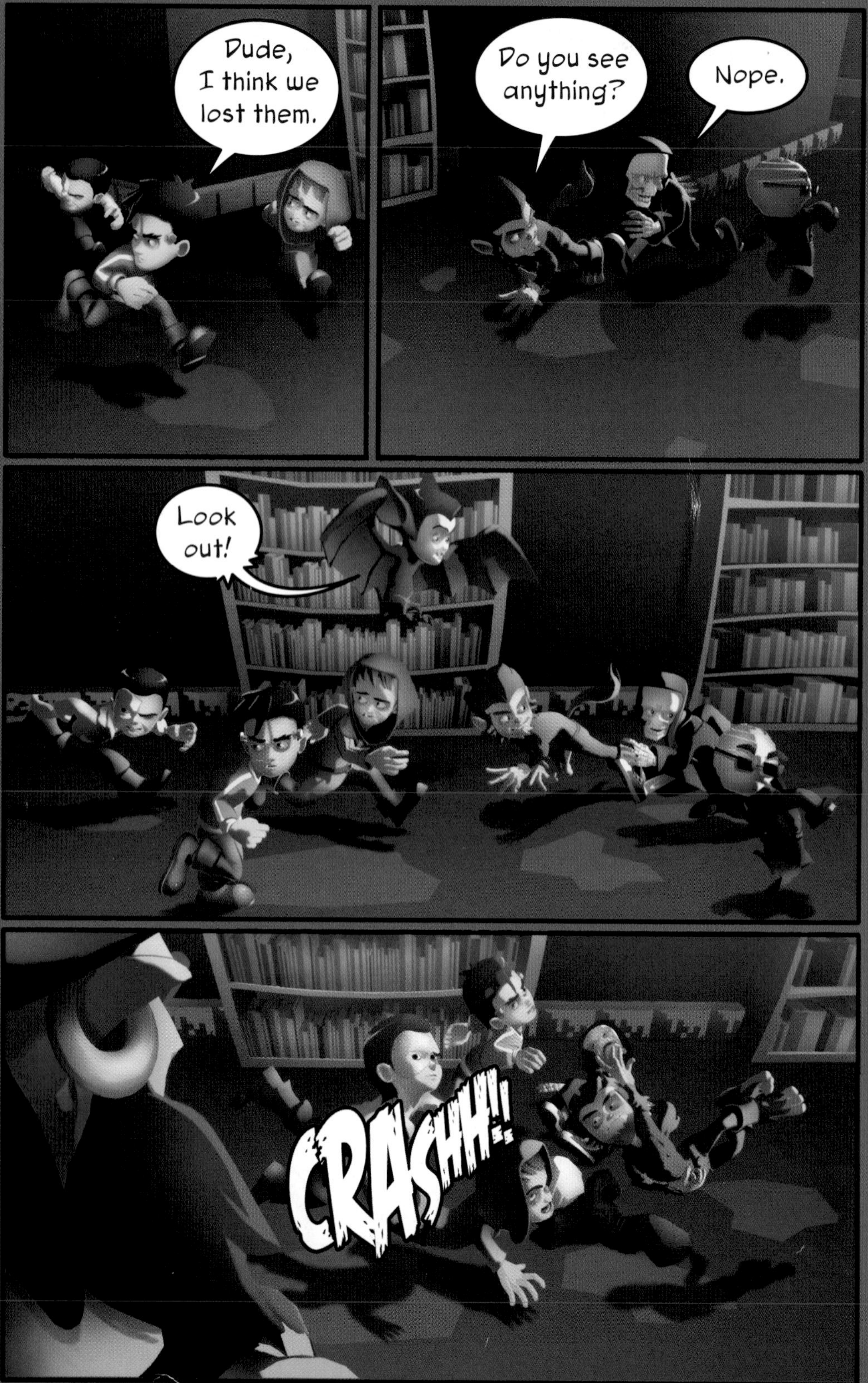
Dude, I think we lost them.
Do you see anything?
Nope.
Look out!
CRASHH!!

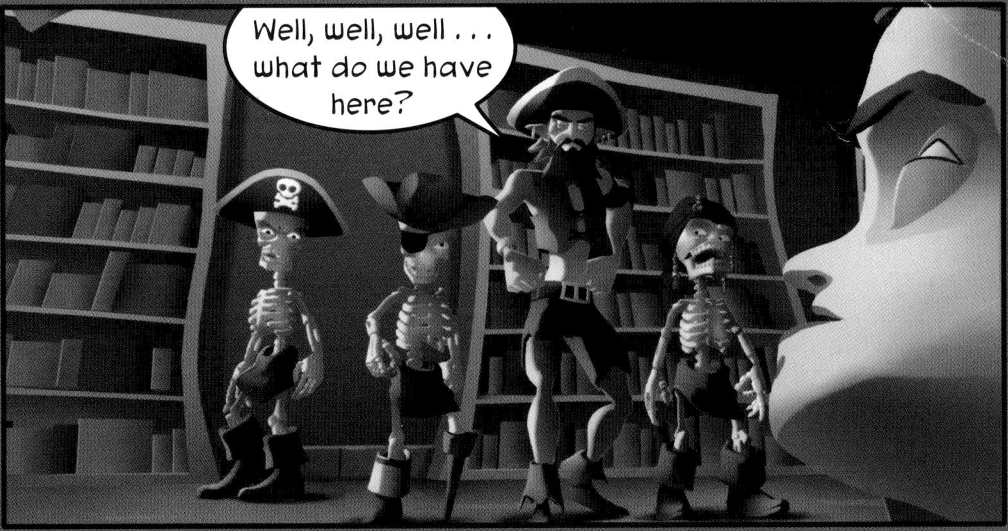
Well, well, well . . . what do we have here?

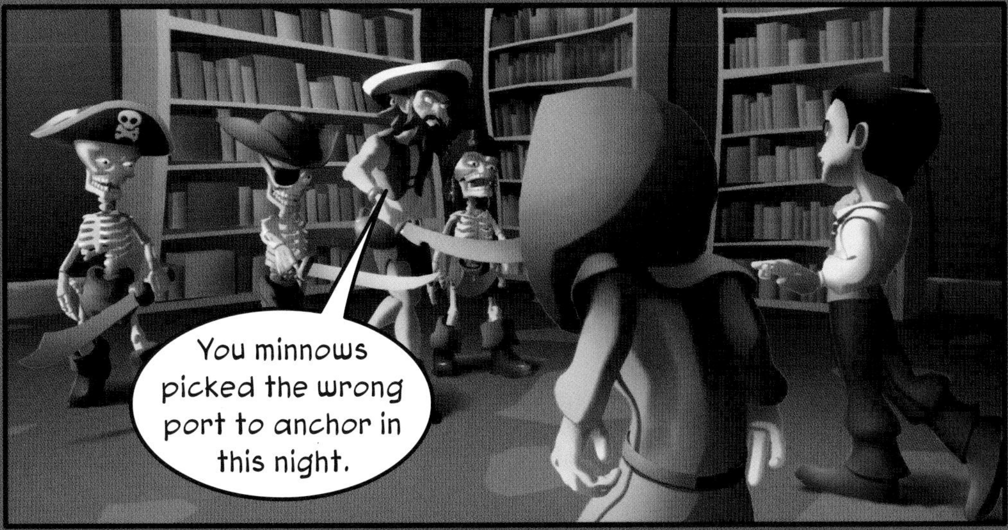
You minnows picked the wrong port to anchor in this night.

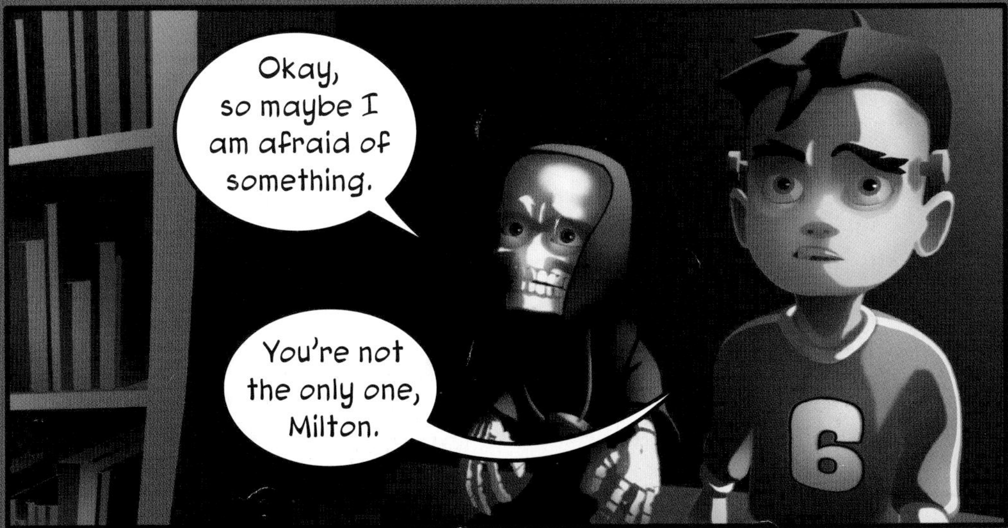
Okay, so maybe I am afraid of something.
You're not the only one, Milton.

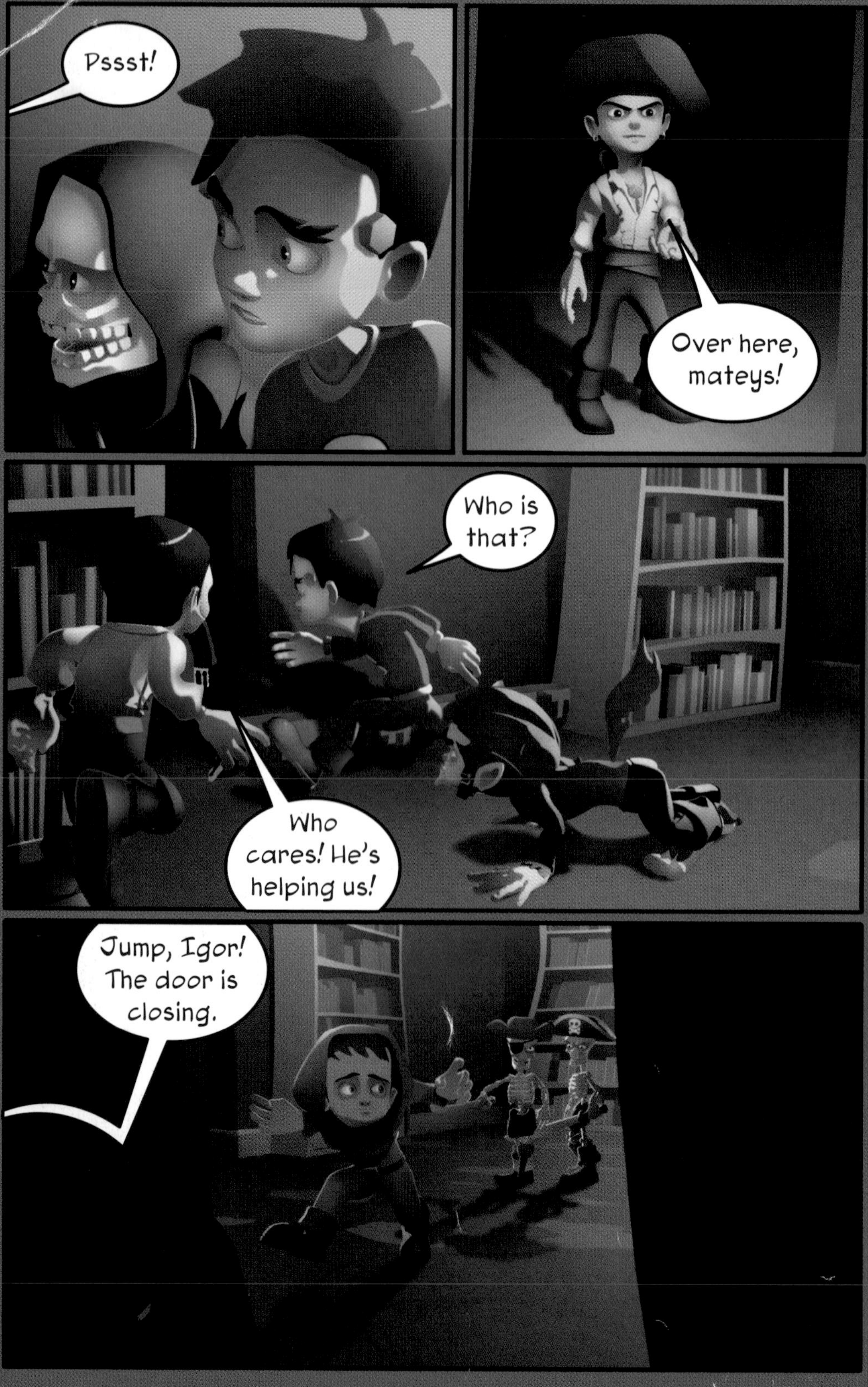
Pssst!
Over here, mateys!
Who is that?
Who cares! He's helping us!
Jump, Igor! The door is closing.

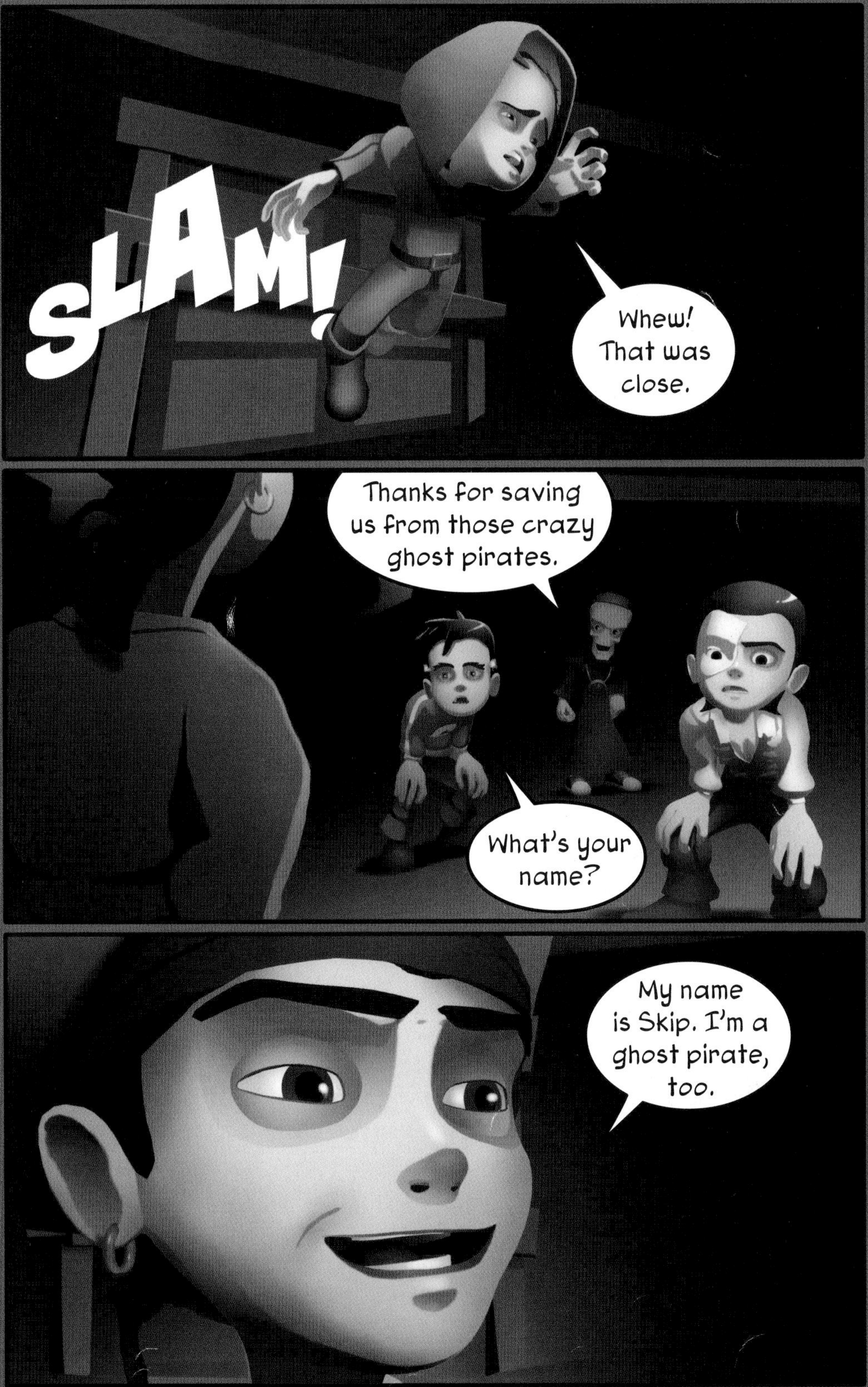
SLAM!
Whew! That was close.
Thanks for saving us from those crazy ghost pirates.
What's your name?
My name is Skip. I'm a ghost pirate, too.

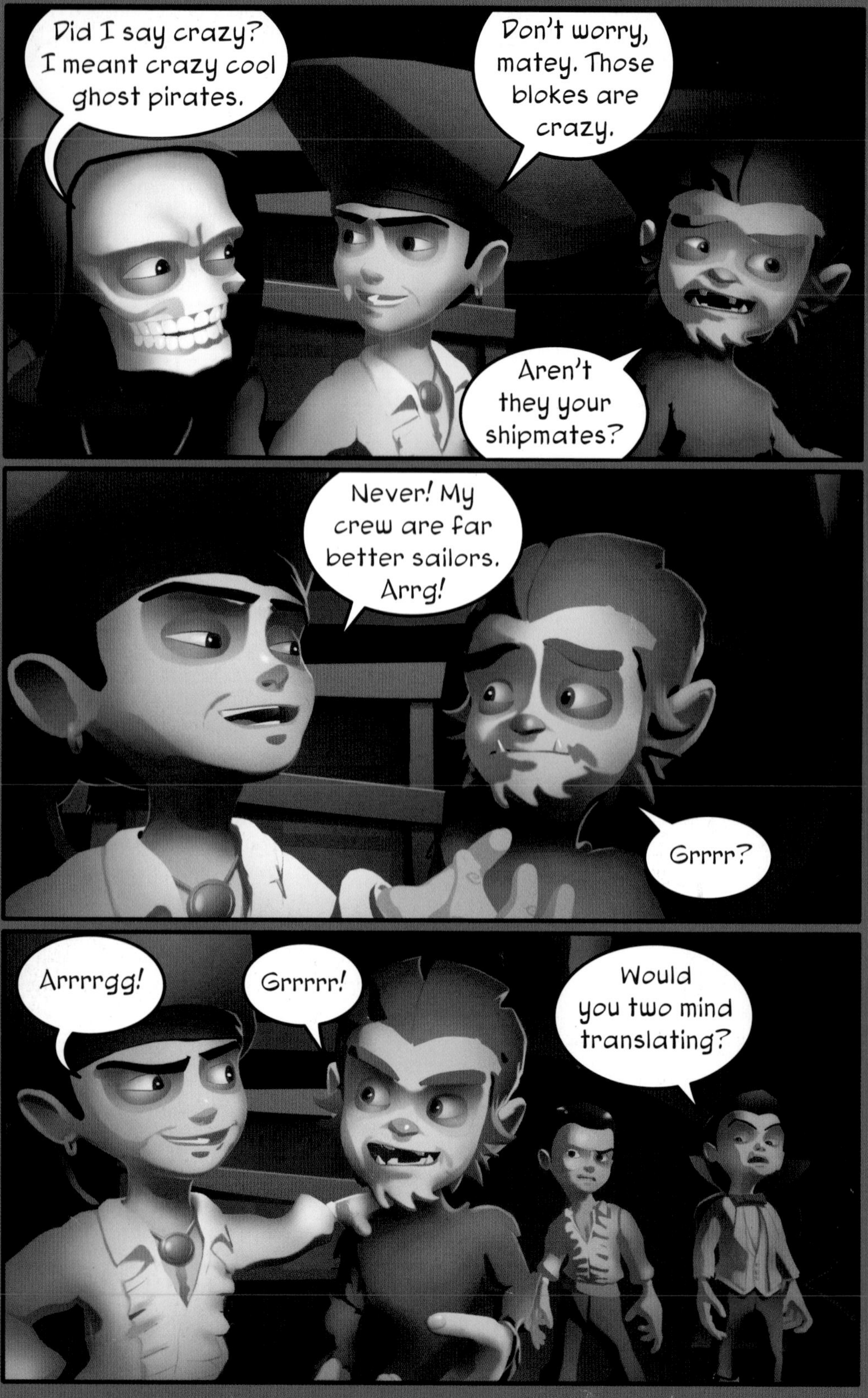
Did I say crazy? I meant crazy cool ghost pirates.
Don't worry, matey. Those blokes are crazy.
Aren't they your shipmates?
Never! My crew are far better sailors. Arrg!
Grrrr?
Arrrrgg!
Grrrrr!
Would you two mind translating?

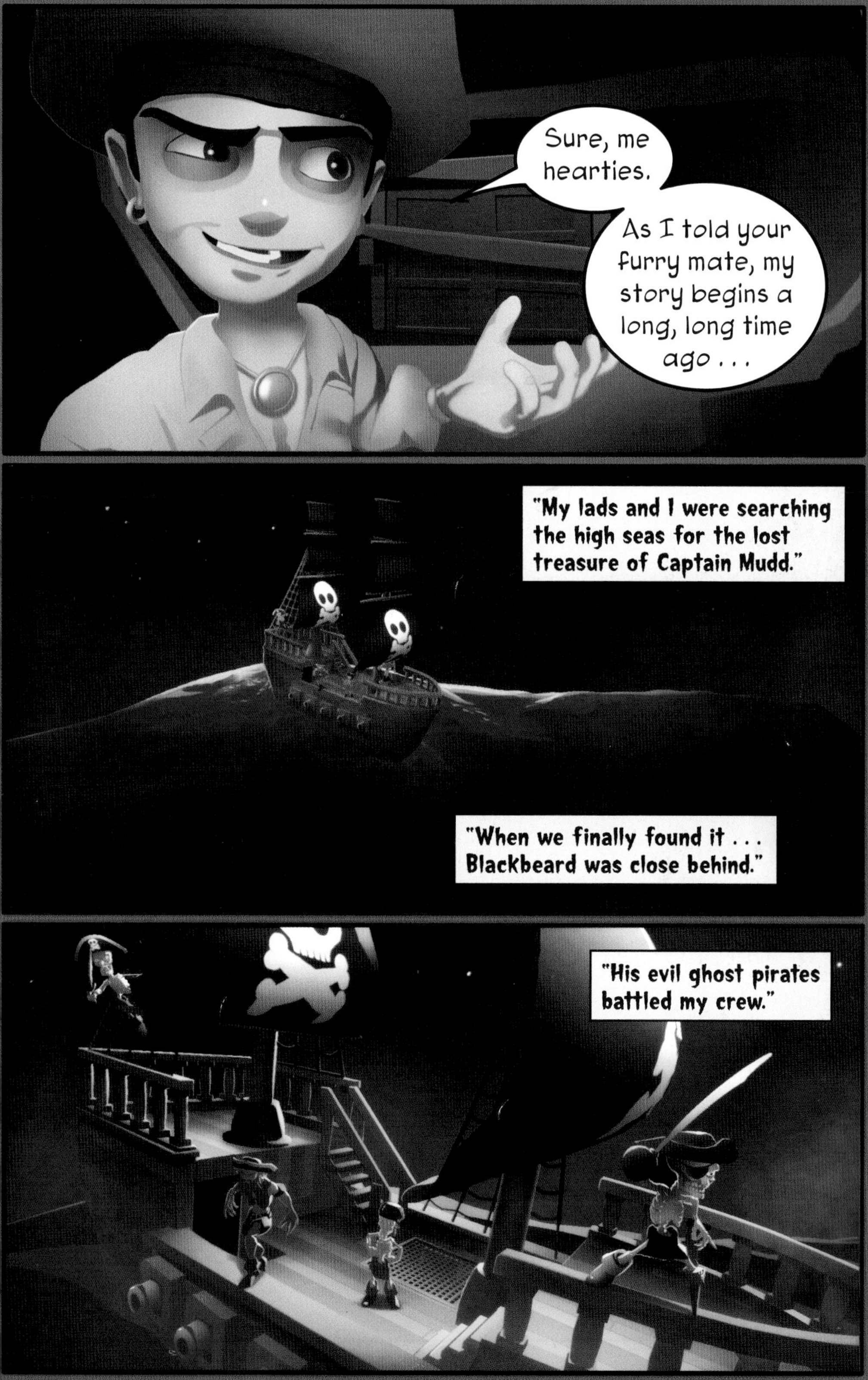
Sure, me hearties.
As I told your furry mate, my story begins a long, long time ago . . .
"My lads and I were searching the high seas for the lost treasure of Captain Mudd."
"When we finally found it . . . Blackbeard was close behind."
"His evil ghost pirates battled my crew."

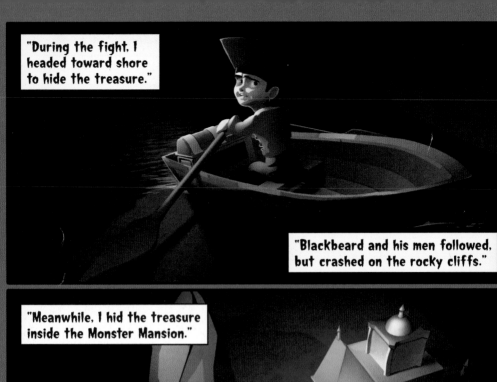

"During the fight, I headed toward shore to hide the treasure."

"Blackbeard and his men followed, but crashed on the rocky cliffs."

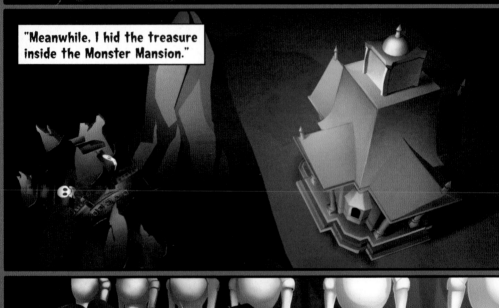

"Meanwhile, I hid the treasure inside the Monster Mansion."

"Since then, I have waited for my crew to return."

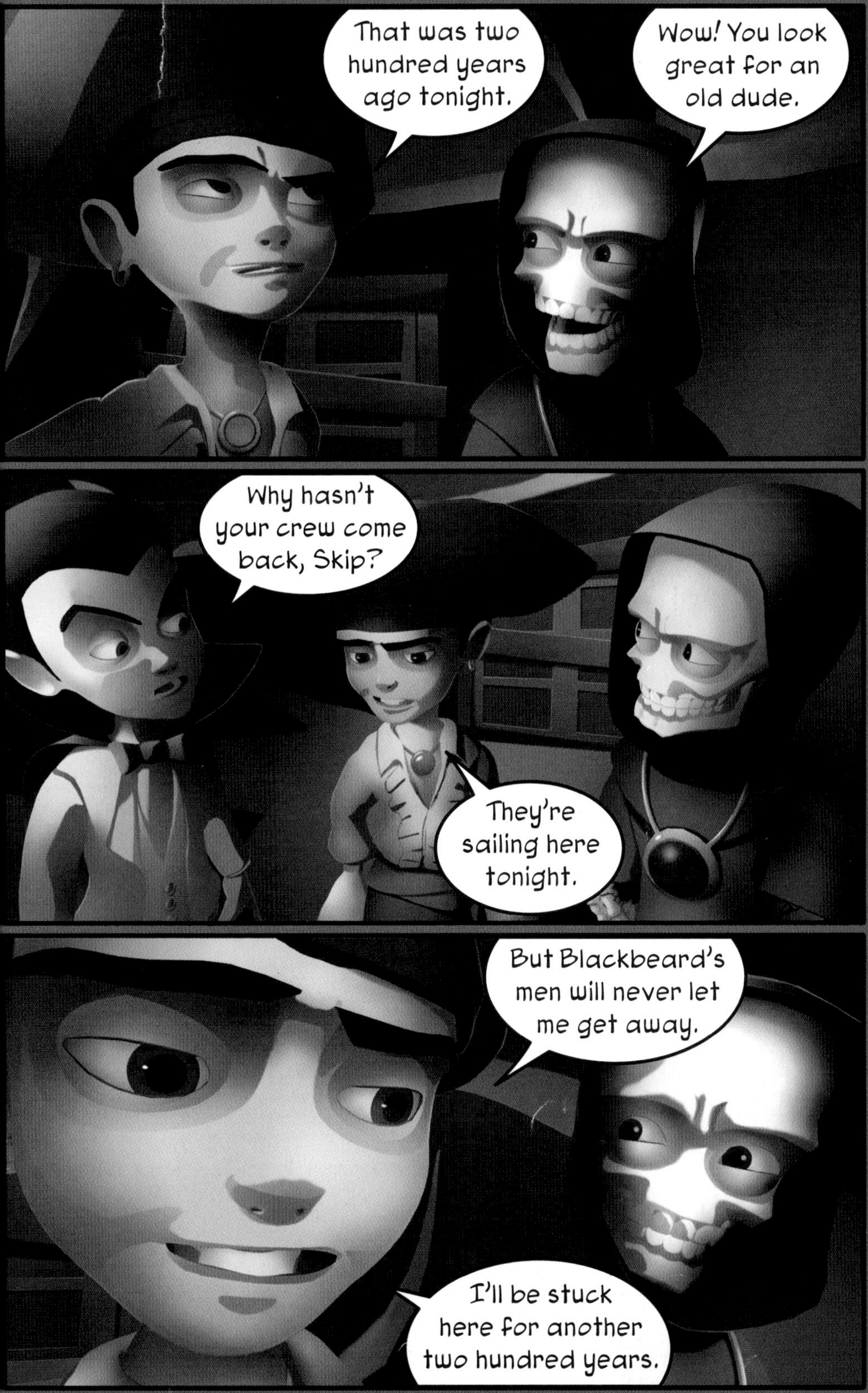
That was two hundred years ago tonight.
Wow! You look great for an old dude.
Why hasn't your crew come back, Skip?
They're sailing here tonight.
But Blackbeard's men will never let me get away.
I'll be stuck here for another two hundred years.

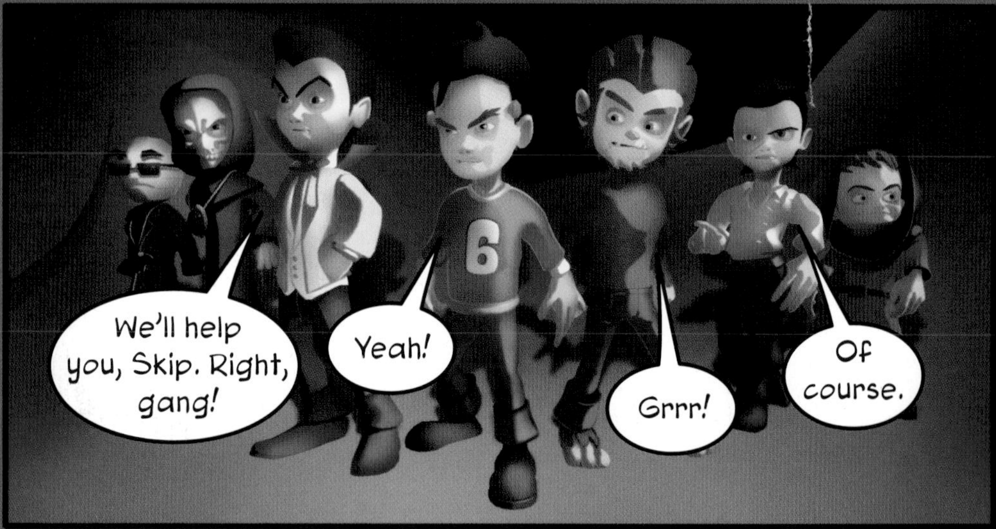
We'll help you, Skip. Right, gang!
Yeah!
Grrr!
Of course.

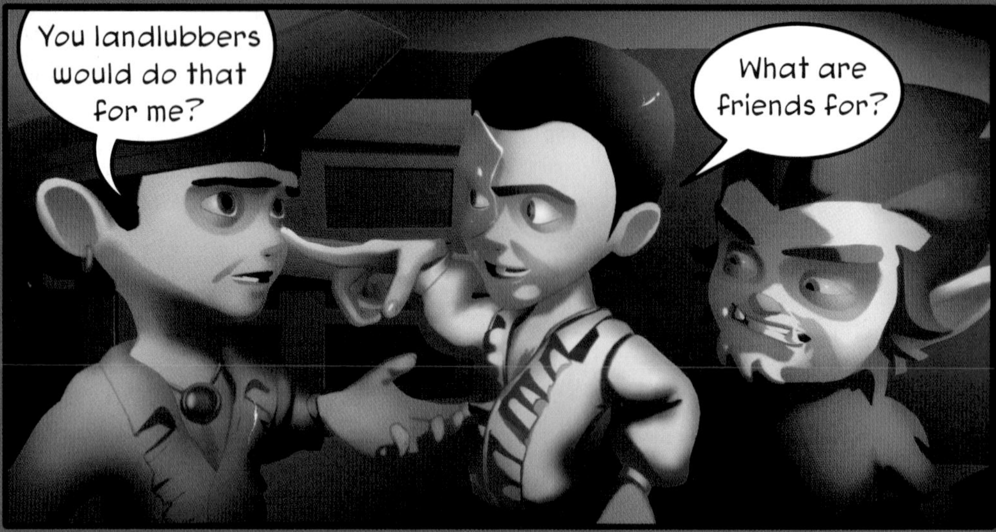
You landlubbers would do that for me?
What are friends for?

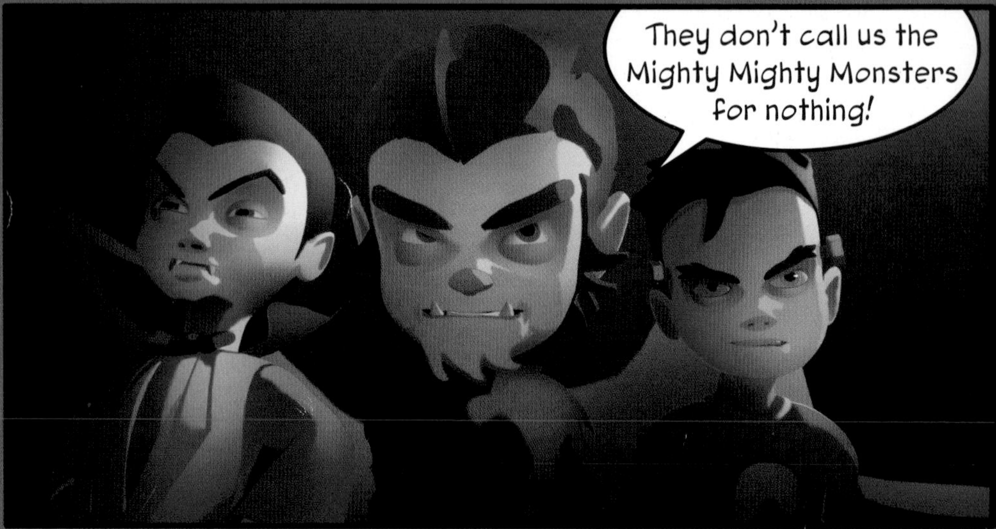
They don't call us the Mighty Mighty Monsters for nothing!

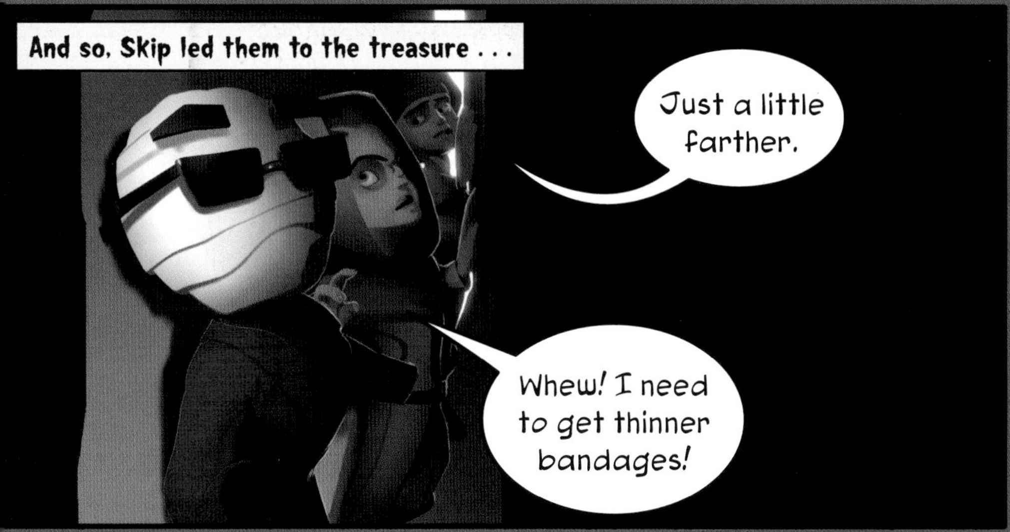
And so, Skip led them to the treasure . . .
Just a little farther.
Whew! I need to get thinner bandages!

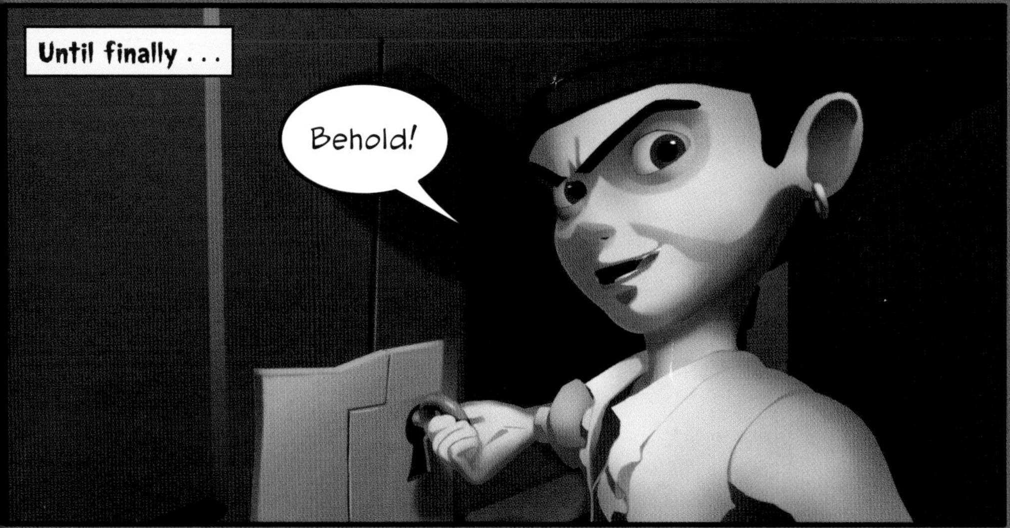
Until finally . . .
Behold!

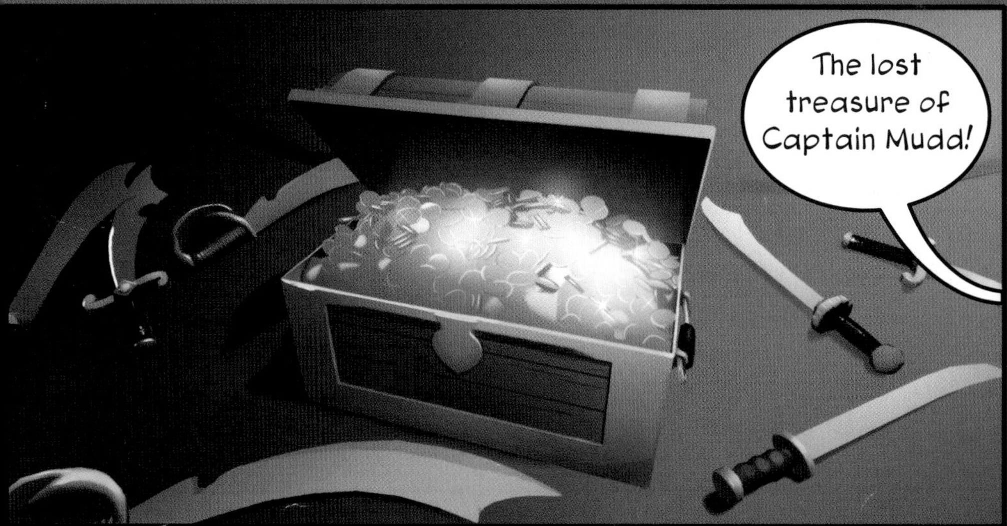
The lost treasure of Captain Mudd!

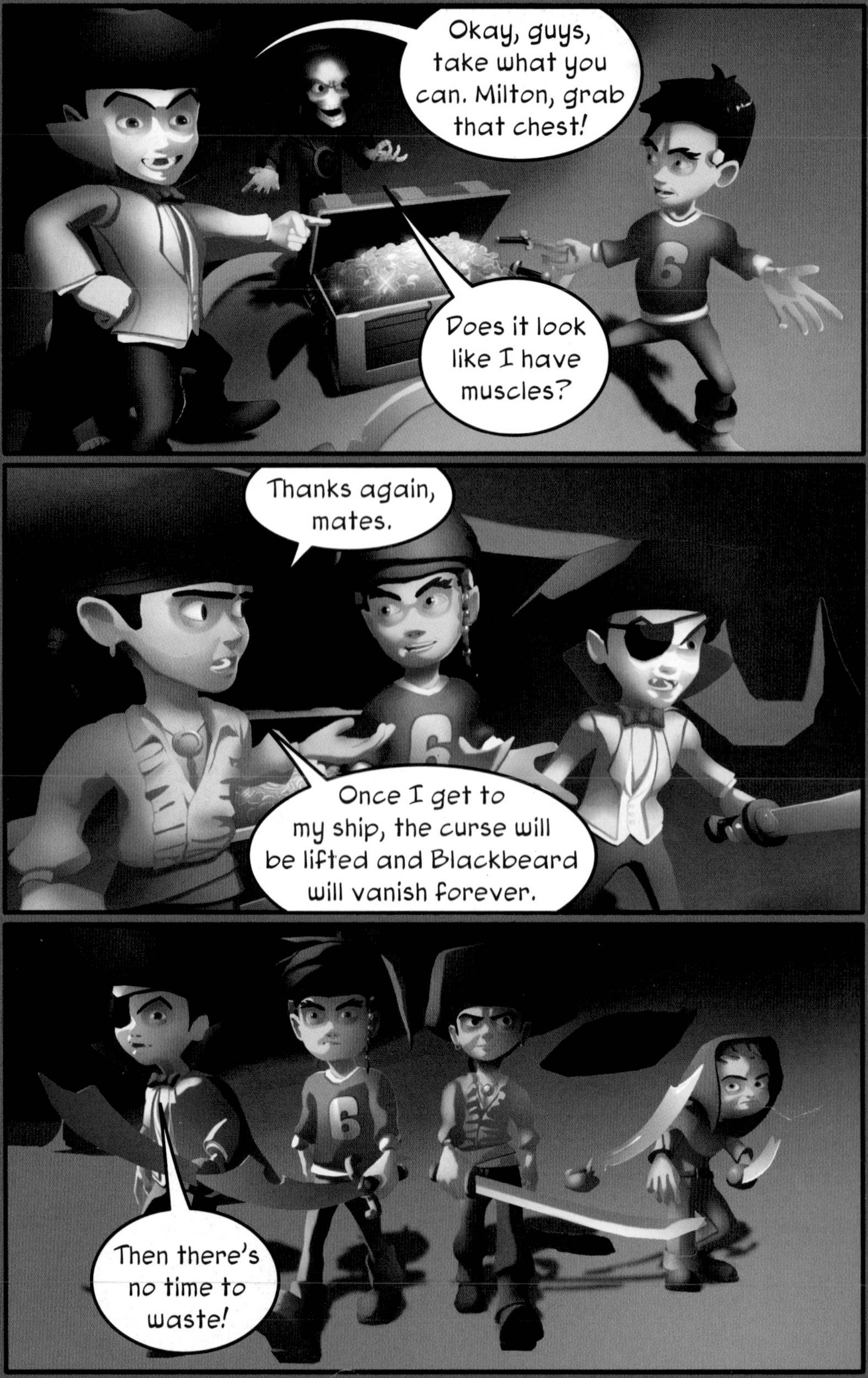
Okay, guys, take what you can. Milton, grab that chest!
Does it look like I have muscles?
Thanks again, mates.
Once I get to my ship, the curse will be lifted and Blackbeard will vanish forever.
Then there's no time to waste!

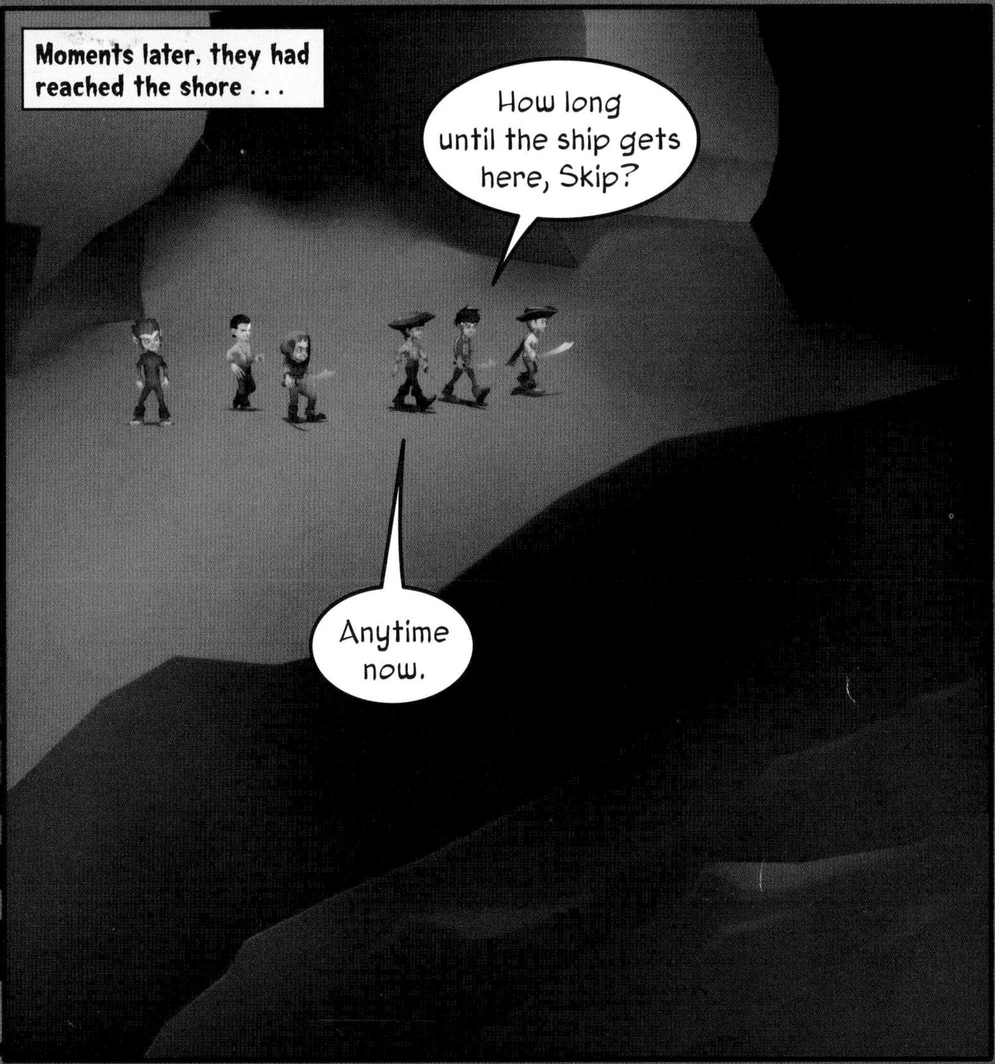
Moments later, they had reached the shore . . .
How long until the ship gets here, Skip?
Anytime now.

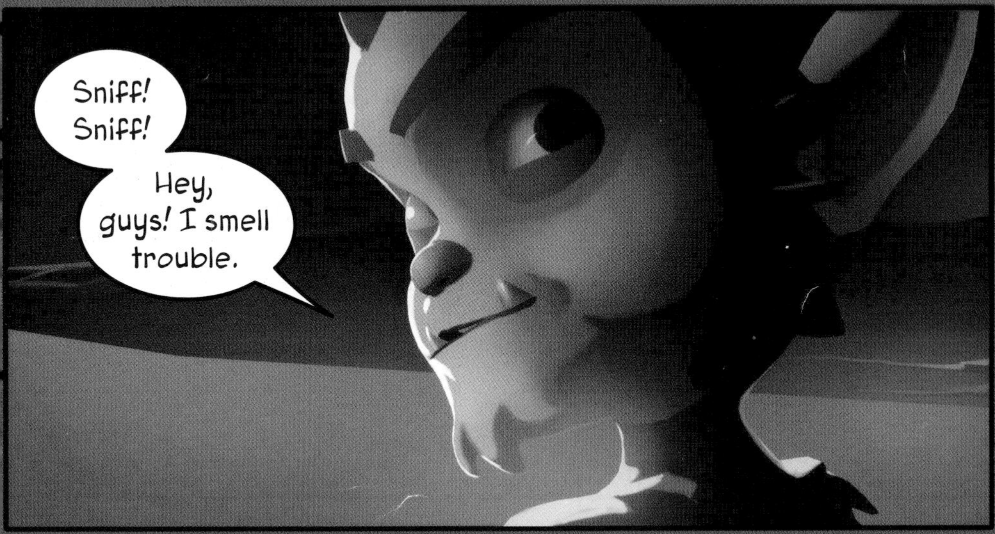
Sniff! Sniff!
Hey, guys! I smell trouble.

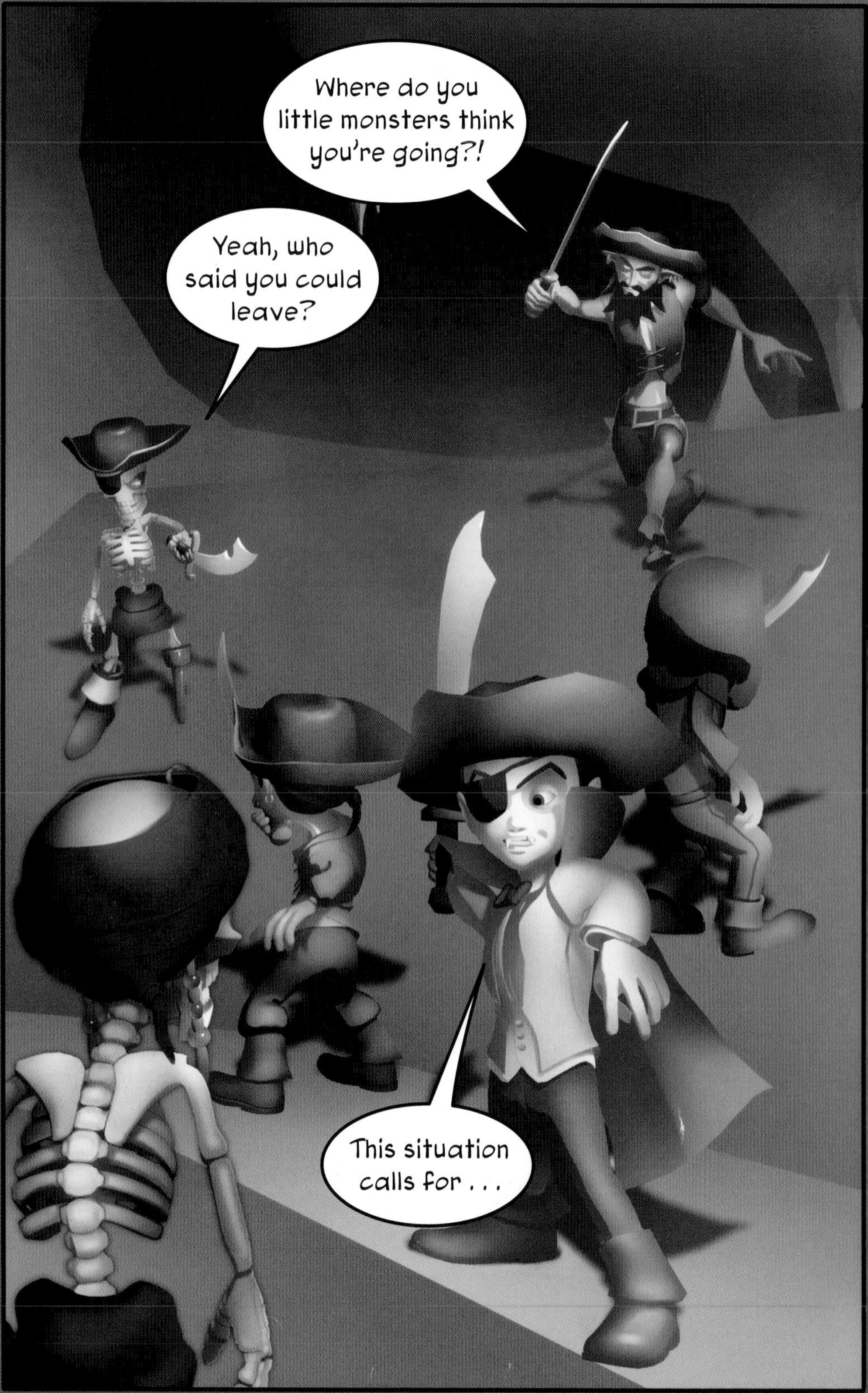
Where do you little monsters think you're going?!
Yeah, who said you could leave?
This situation calls for . . .

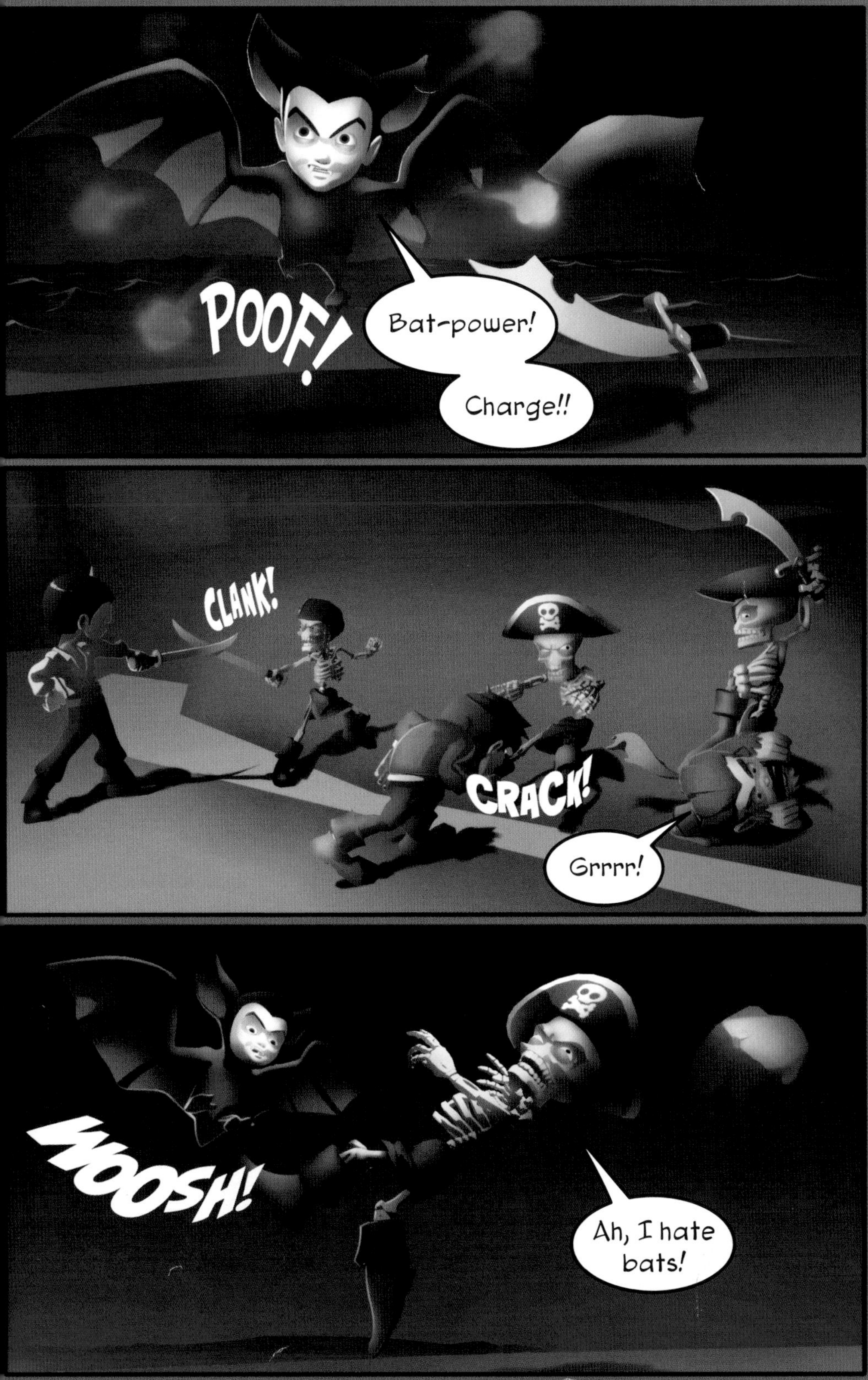
POOF!
Bat-power!
Charge!!
CLANK!
CRACK!
Grrrr!
WOOSH!
Ah, I hate bats!

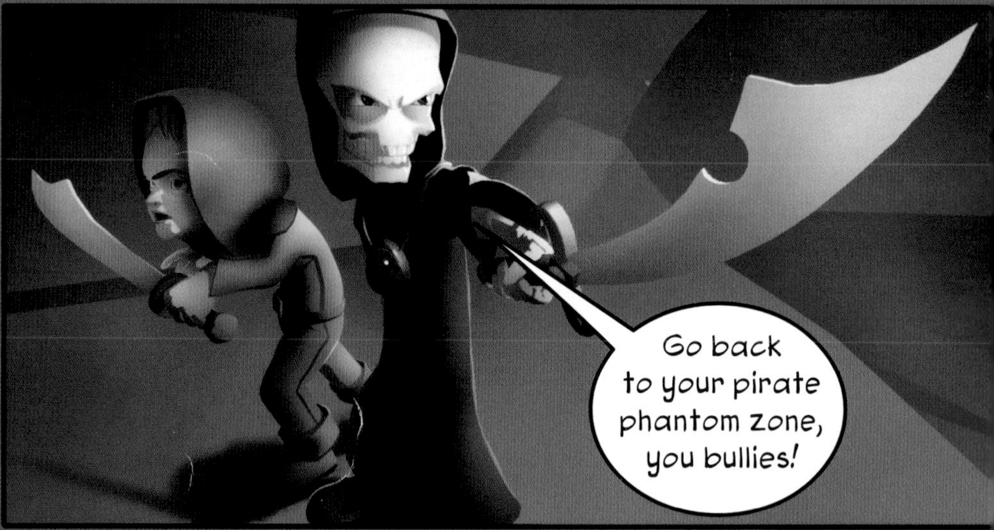
Go back to your pirate phantom zone, you bullies!

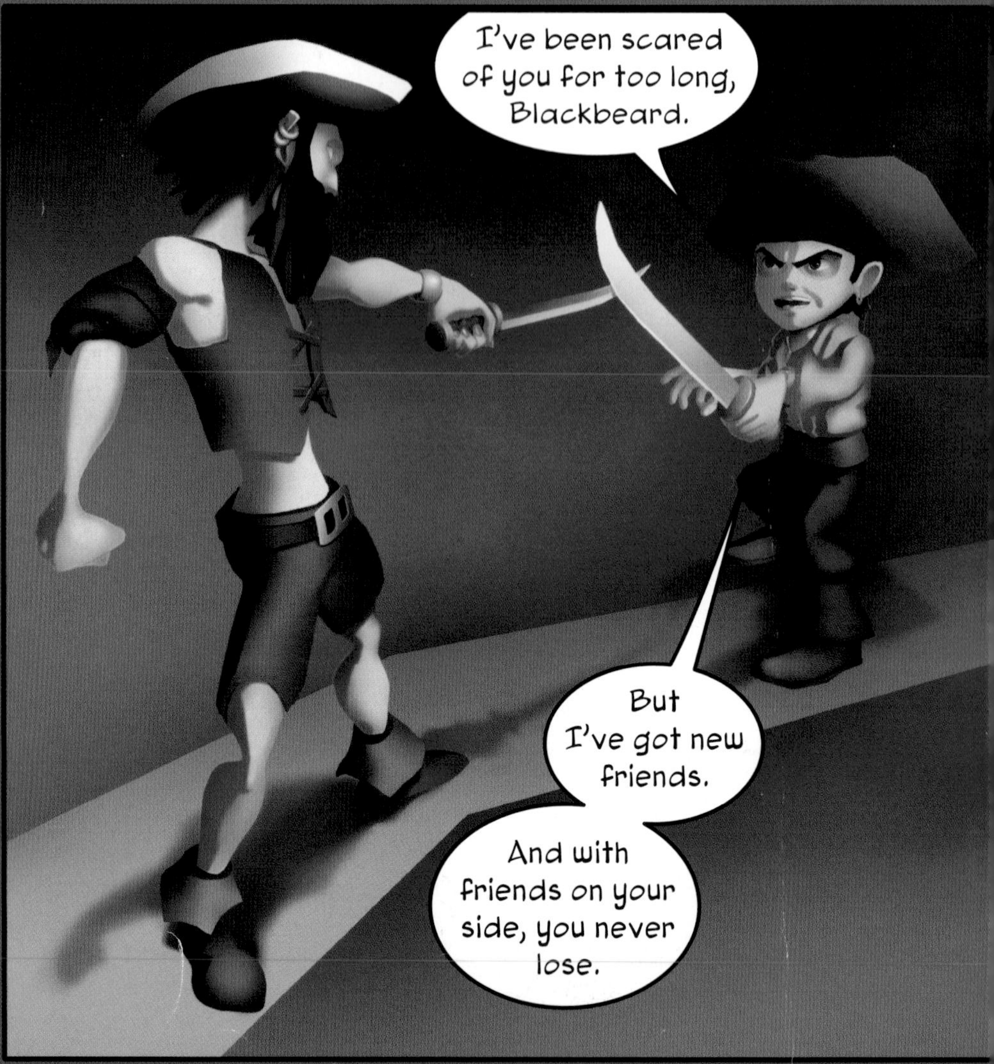
I've been scared of you for too long, Blackbeard.
But I've got new friends.
And with friends on your side, you never lose.

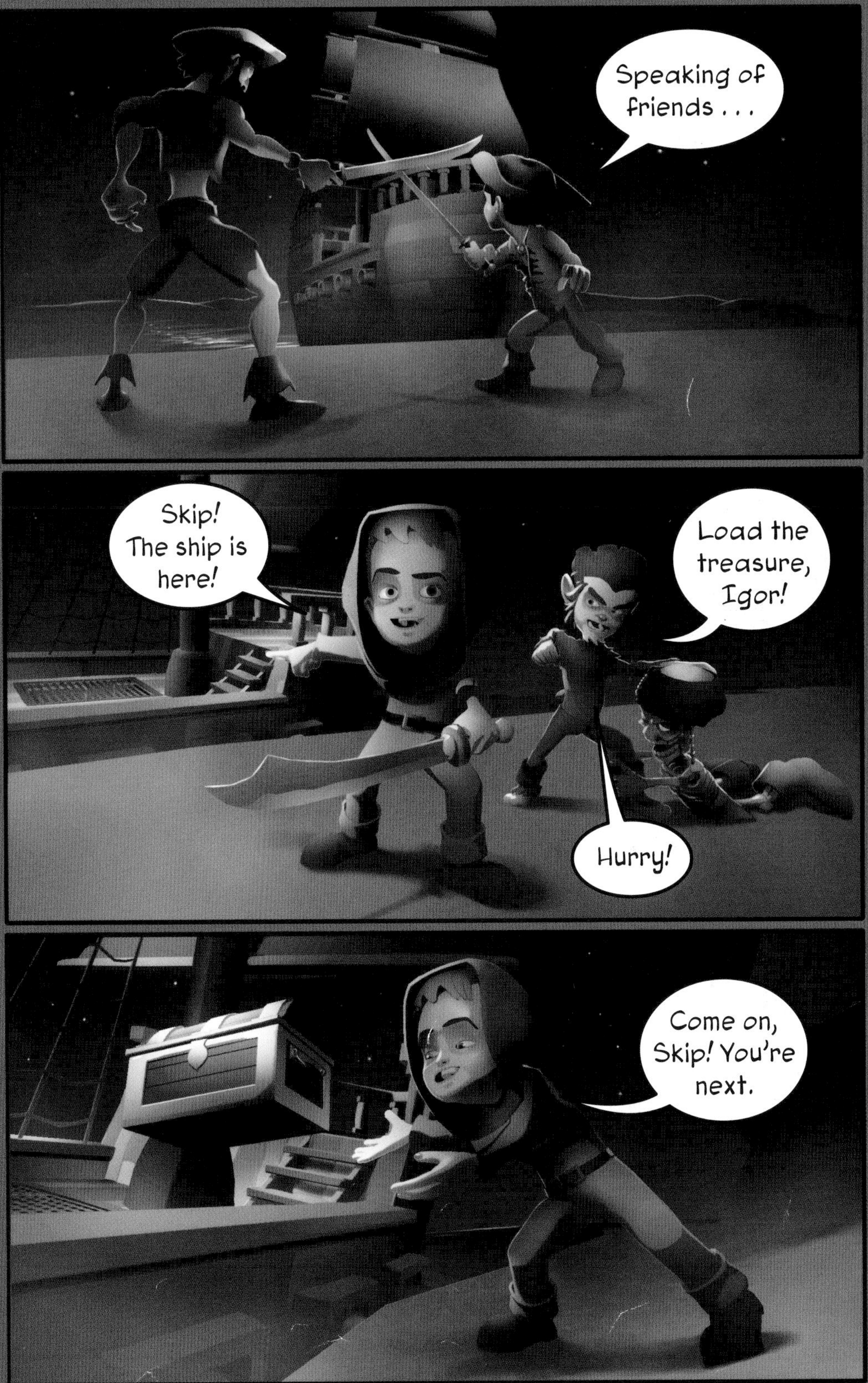
Speaking of friends . . .
Skip! The ship is here!
Load the treasure, Igor!
Hurry!
Come on, Skip! You're next.

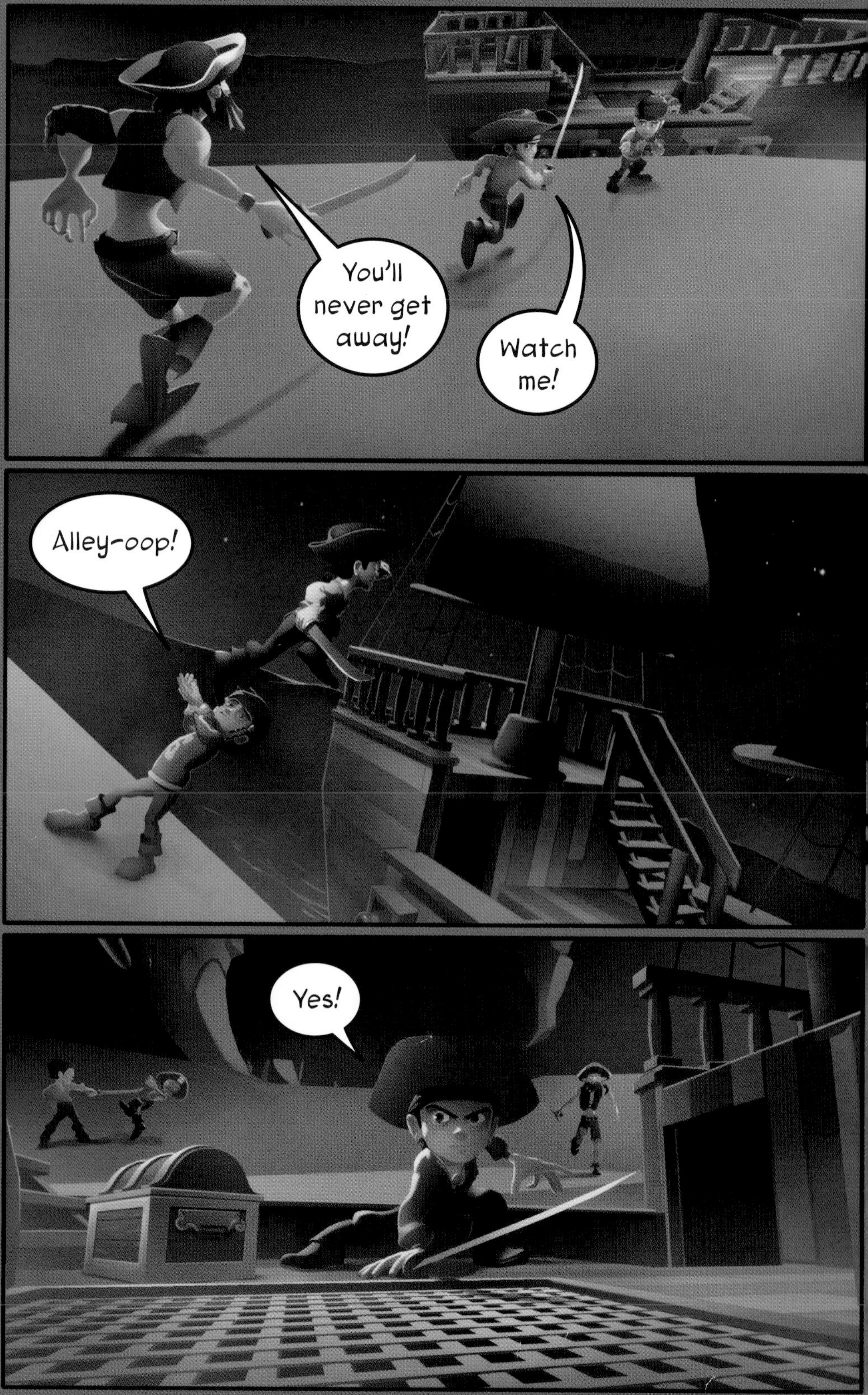
You'll never get away!
Watch me!
Alley-oop!
Yes!

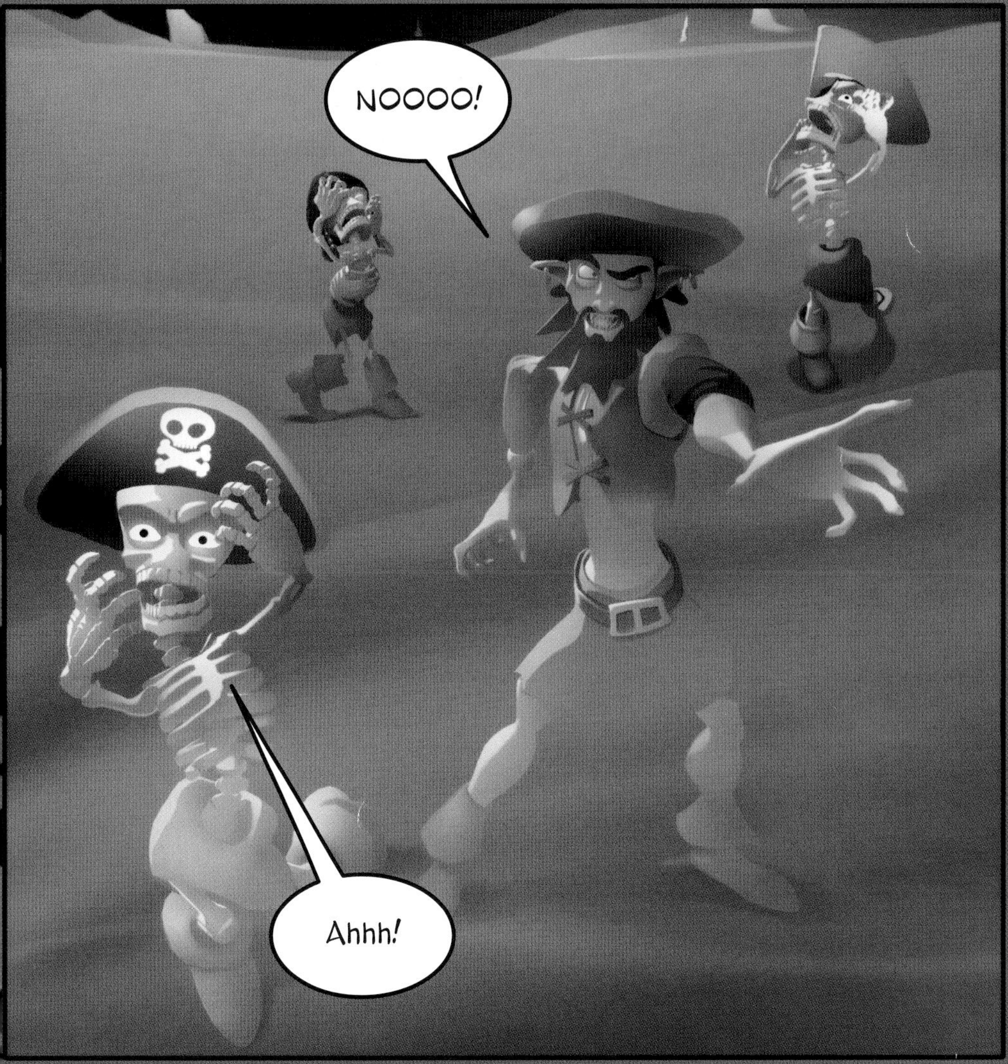
NOOOO!
Ahhh!

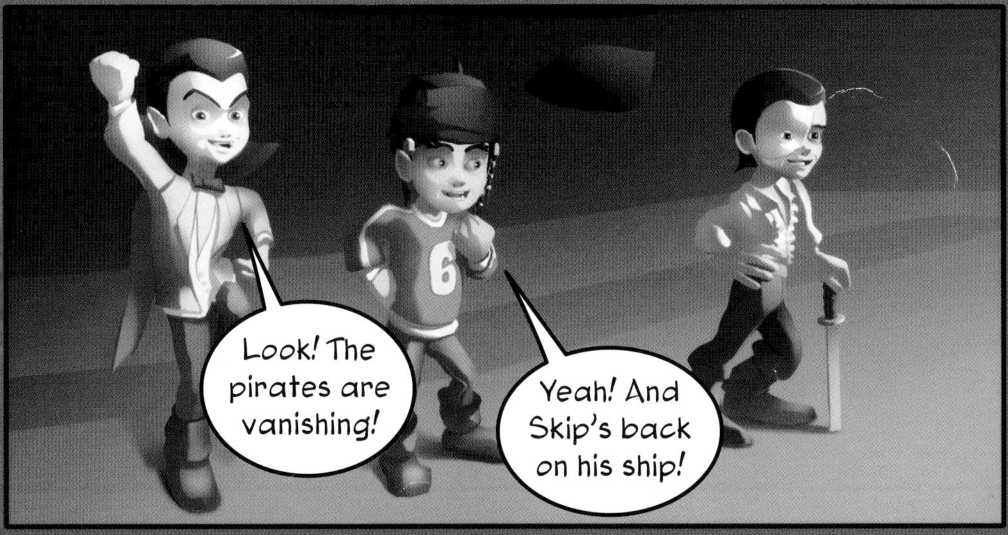
Look! The pirates are vanishing!
Yeah! And Skip's back on his ship!

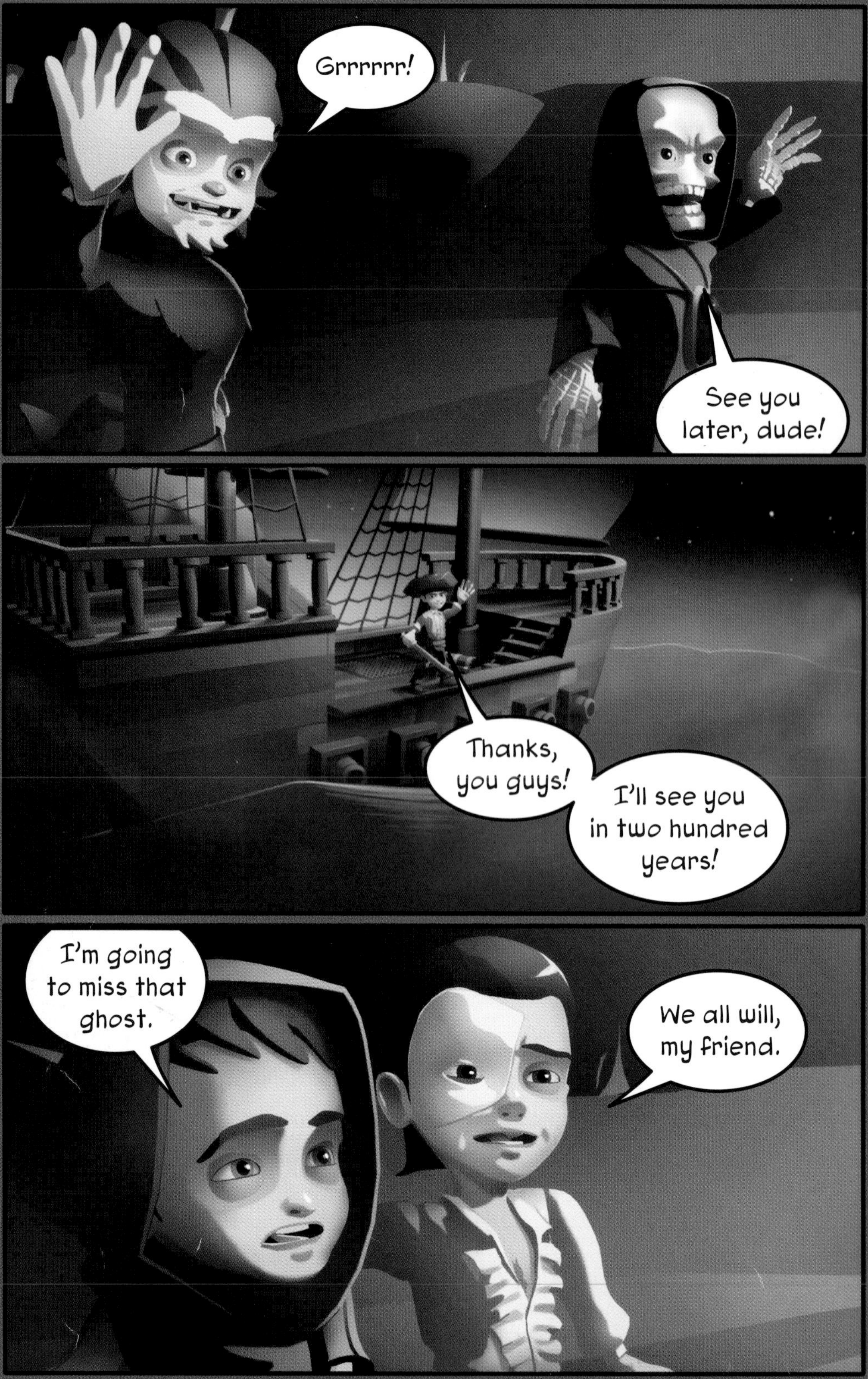
Grrrrrr!
See you later, dude!
Thanks, you guys!
I'll see you in two hundred years!
I'm going to miss that ghost.
We all will, my friend.

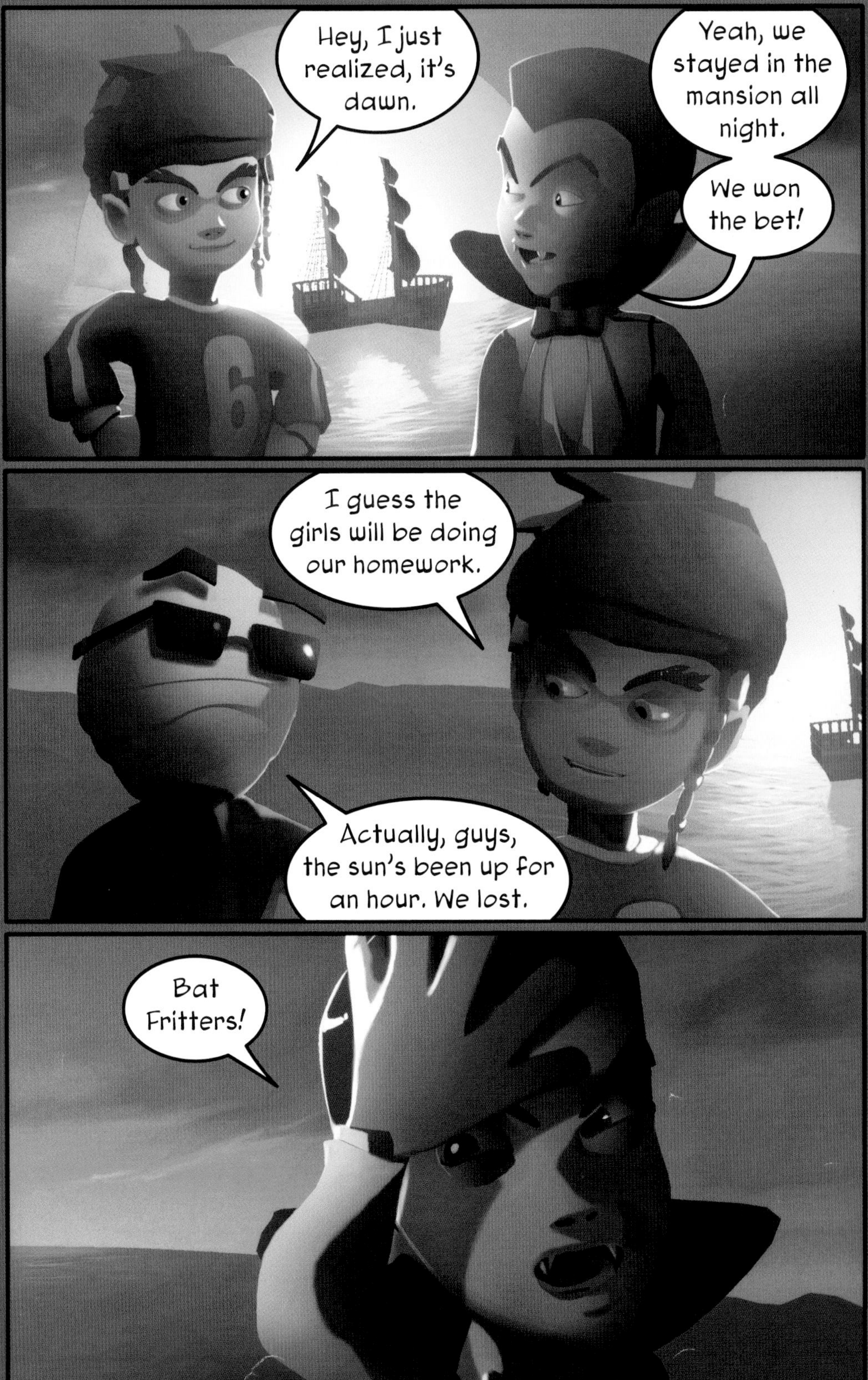
Hey, I just realized, it's dawn.
Yeah, we stayed in the mansion all night.
We won the bet!
I guess the girls will be doing our homework.
Actually, guys, the sun's been up for an hour. We lost.
Bat Fritters!

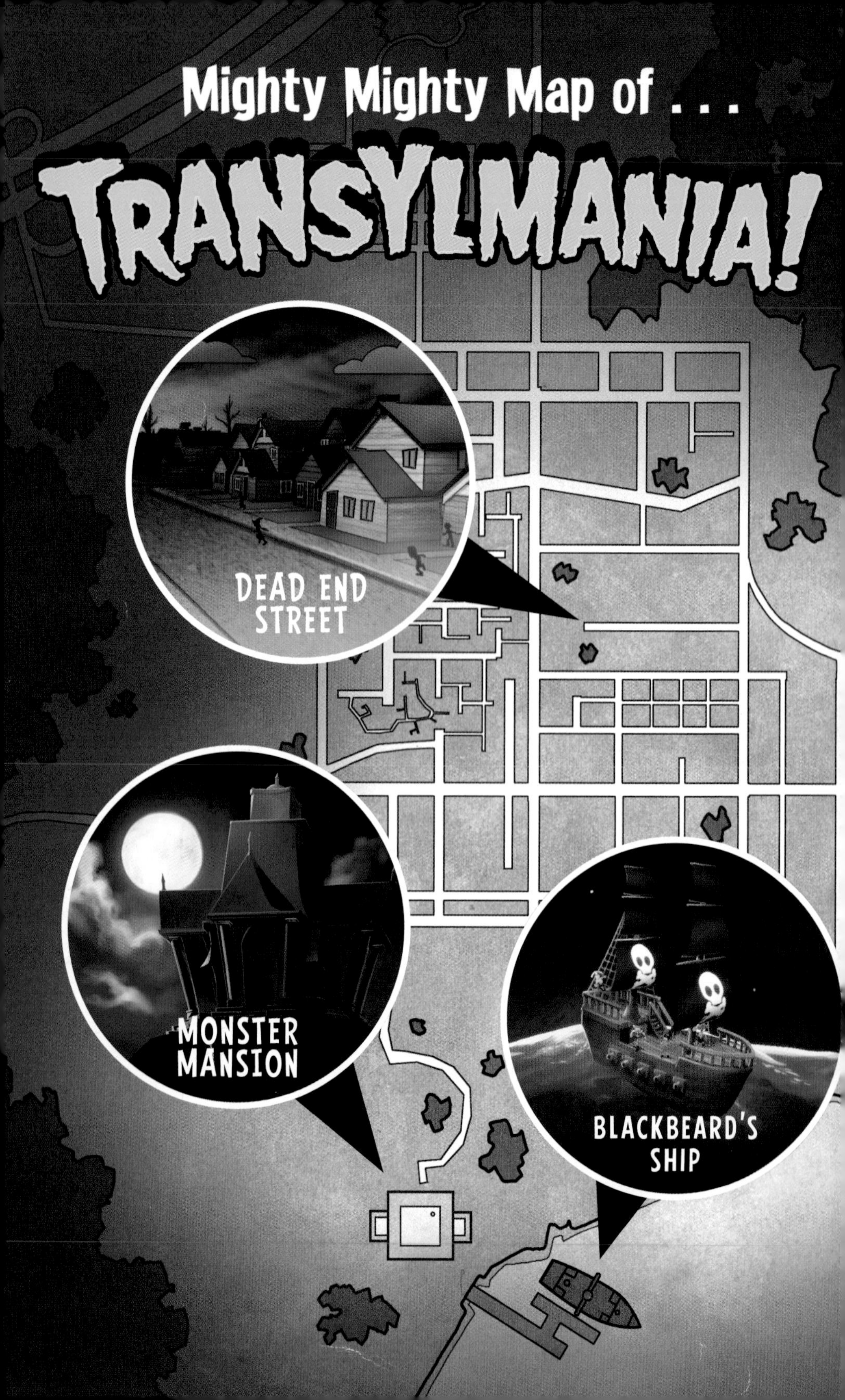
Mighty Mighty Map of . . .
TRANSYLMANIA!
DEAD END
STREET
MONSTER
MANSION
BLACKBEARD'S
SHIP

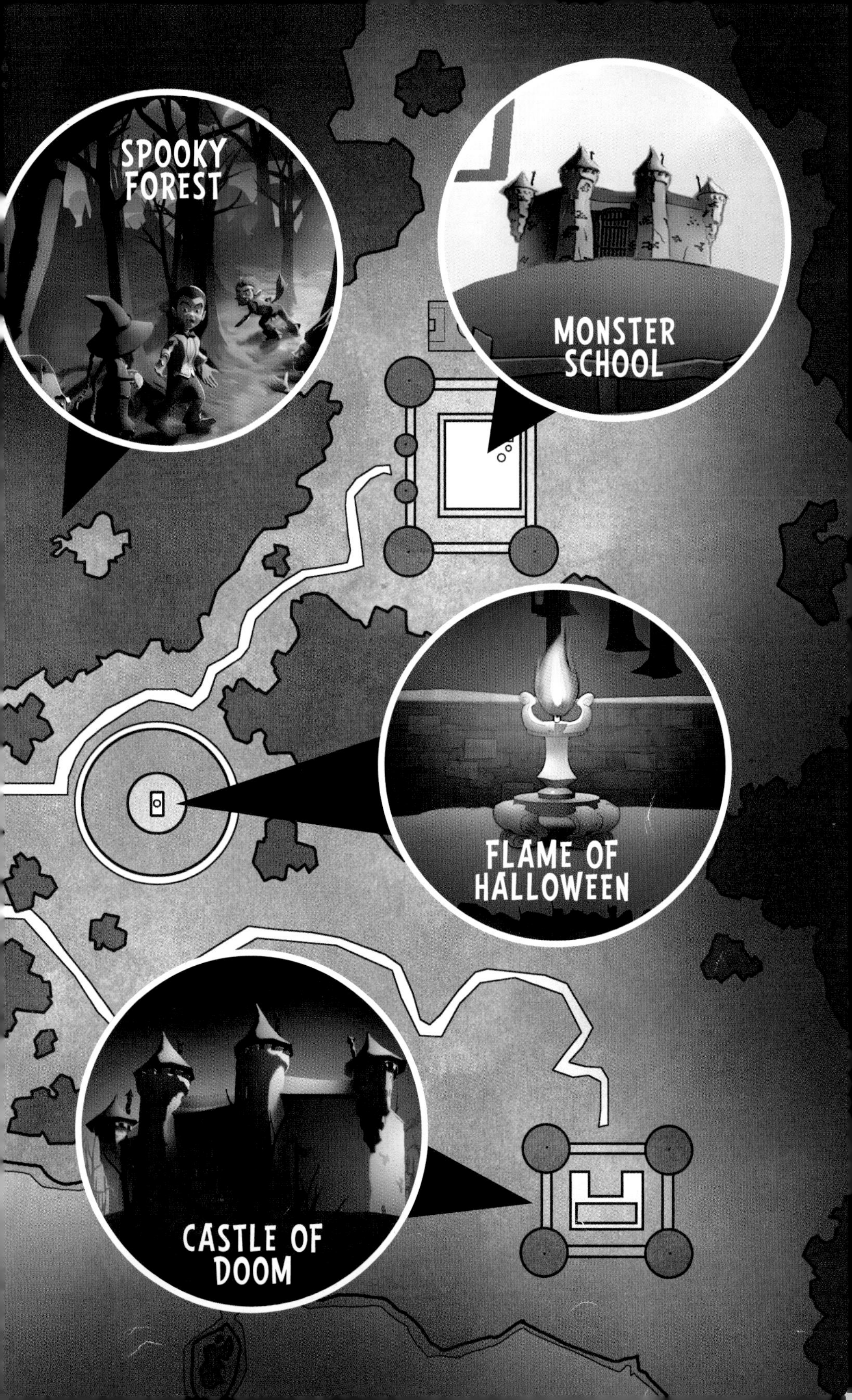
SPOOKY FOREST
MONSTER SCHOOL
FLAME OF HALLOWEEN
CASTLE OF DOOM

Mighty Mighty MONSTERS

...BEFORE THEY WERE STARS!

Igor

Nickname: Hunchie

Hometown: Transylmania

Favorite Color: Green

Favorite Animal: Camels

Mighty Mighty Powers: Super sixth sense; his "hunches" are never wrong; small enough to fit into tiny spaces.

BIOGRAPHY

Orphaned at birth, Igor often struggled to fit in at school . . . until he met the Mighty Mighty Monsters! These fearsome friends quickly adopted him into their creepy crew. And, although he remained shy, the young hunchback brought a special set of skills to the ghoulish gang. His "hunches" were never wrong, and he always steered the Mighty Mighty Monsters the right way. With a clear sense of direction, a keen intuition, and a unique style, it's no wonder he became a monster icon.

WHERE ARE THEY NOW?

Many people believe Igor first appeared in the 1931 movie *Frankenstein*. However, that hunchback was actually named "Fritz." The character "Ygor" did not appear until the movie *Son of Frankenstein* in 1938.

In the *Son of Frankenstein*, Bela Lugosi played the role of Ygor, Dr. Frankenstein's hunchbacked assistant. The actor had already gained fame playing Dracula in the 1931 movie.

Other famous hunchback characters include Quasimodo, featured in the 1831 novel *The Hunchback of Notre-Dame*. Disney made the story into a popular animated movie in 1996.

ABOUT SEAN O'REILLY
AND ARCANA STUDIO

As a lifelong comics fan, Sean O'Reilly dreamed of becoming a comic book creator. In 2004, he realized that dream by creating Arcana Studio. In one short year, O'Reilly took his studio from a one-person operation in his basement to an award-winning comic book publisher with more than 150 graphic novels produced for Harper Collins, Simon & Schuster, Random House, Scholastic, and others.

Within a year, the company won many awards including the Shuster Award for Outstanding Publisher and the Moonbeam Award for top children's graphic novel. O'Reilly also won the Top 40 Under 40 award from the city of Vancouver and authored *The Clockwork Girl* for Top Graphic Novel at Book Expo America in 2009.

Currently, O'Reilly is one of the most prolific independent comic book writers in Canada. While showing no signs of slowing down in comics, he now writes screenplays and adapts his creations for the big screen.

GLOSSARY

calcium (KAL-see-uhm)—a soft, silver-white chemical element found in teeth and bones

dawn (DAWN)—the beginning of the day; sunrise.

hunch (HUHNCH)—an idea that is not backed by proof but comes from a feeling

manners (MAN-urz)—polite behavior

mansion (MAN-shuhn)—a very large and grand house

mate (MATE)—a friend

mood (MOOD)—the way a person is feeling

neighbor (NAY-bur)—someone who lives next door to you or near you

phantom zone (FAN-tom ZOHN)—an area where ghosts live

translate (TRANZ-late)—to express in a different language

tutor (TOO-tur)—a teacher who gives private lessons to one student at a time

vanish (VAN-ish)—to disappear suddenly

DISCUSSION QUESTIONS

1. Igor warned the other Mighty Mighty Monsters not to go inside the mansion. Should they have listened to him? Why or why not?

2. Skip was a ghost pirate. Why did the Mighty Mighty Monsters decide to help him?

3. All of the Mighty Mighty Monsters are different. Which character do you like the best? Why?

WRITING PROMPTS

1. The Mighty Mighty Monsters are based on classic movie monsters including Frankenstein, Dracula, and the Wolfman. Write your own story using one of these creepy characters.

2. Write your own Mighty Mighty Monsters adventure. What will the ghoulish gang do next? What villains will they face? You decide.

3. In this story, the Mighty Mighty Monsters helped out a new friend. Describe a time that you helped a friend or family member.

Mighty Mighty MONSTERS ADVENTURES

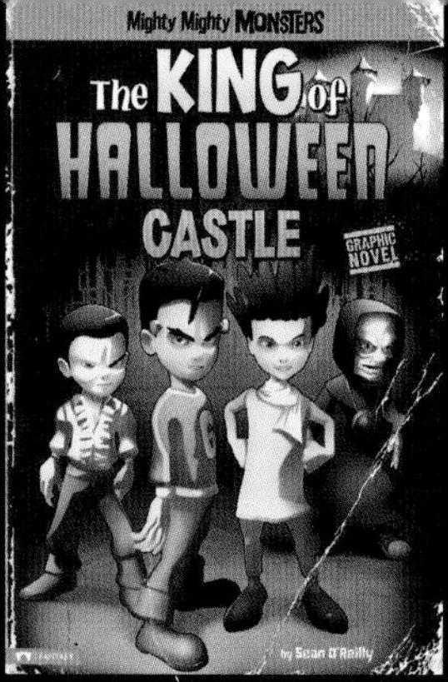
Mighty Mighty MONSTERS
The KING of HALLOWEEN CASTLE
GRAPHIC NOVEL
by Sean O'Reilly

The King of Halloween Castle

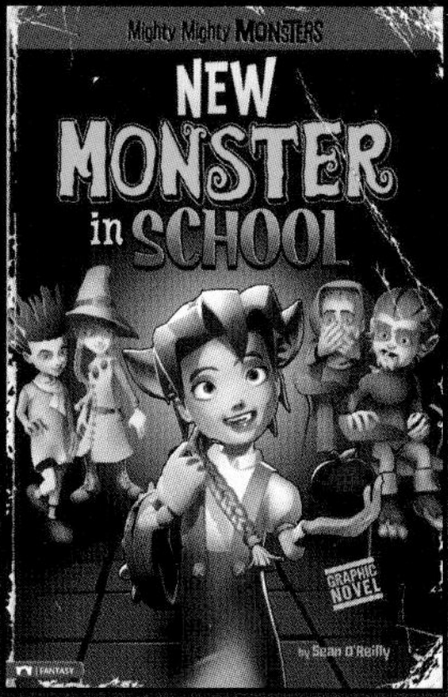
Mighty Mighty MONSTERS
NEW MONSTER in SCHOOL
GRAPHIC NOVEL
by Sean O'Reilly

New Monster in School

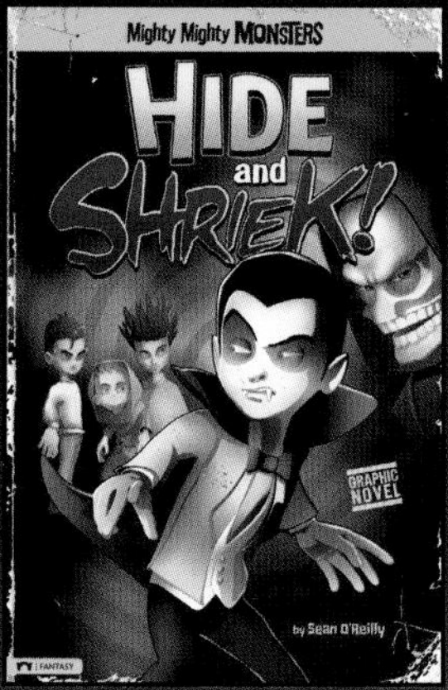
Mighty Mighty MONSTERS
HIDE and SHRIEK!
GRAPHIC NOVEL
by Sean O'Reilly

Hide and Shriek

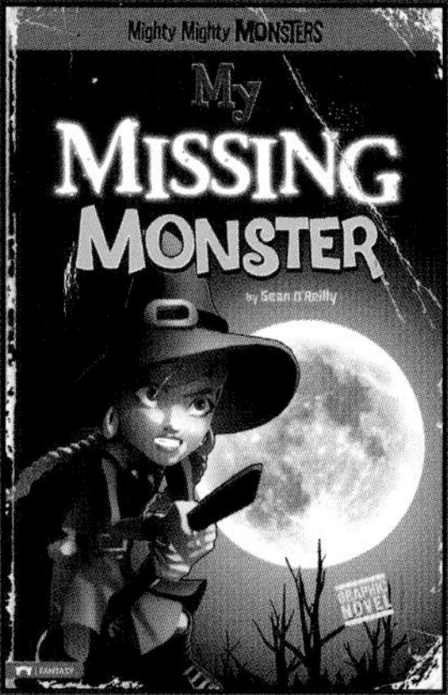
Mighty Mighty MONSTERS
My MISSING MONSTER
by Sean O'Reilly
GRAPHIC NOVEL

My Missing Monster

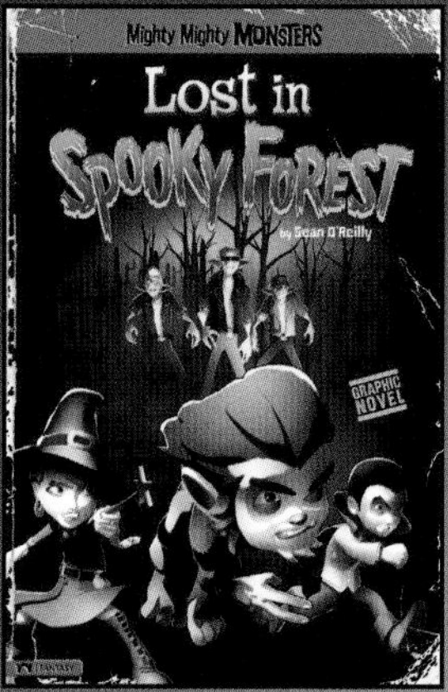
Mighty Mighty MONSTERS
Lost in SPOOKY FOREST
by Sean O'Reilly
GRAPHIC NOVEL

Lost in Spooky Forest

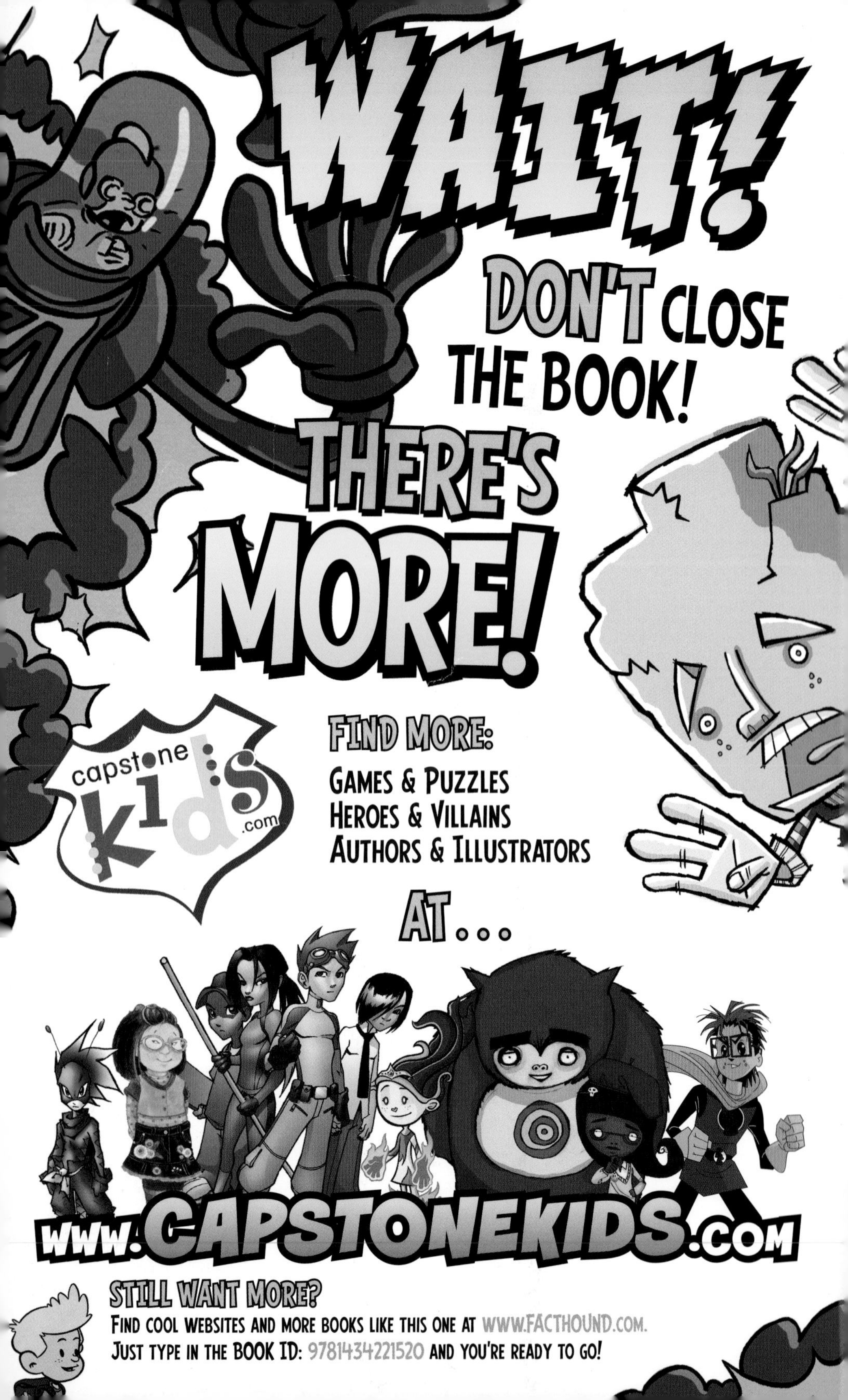
WAIT!
DON'T CLOSE THE BOOK!
THERE'S MORE!
capstone kids .com
FIND MORE:
GAMES & PUZZLES
HEROES & VILLAINS
AUTHORS & ILLUSTRATORS
AT...
WWW.CAPSTONEKIDS.COM
STILL WANT MORE?
FIND COOL WEBSITES AND MORE BOOKS LIKE THIS ONE AT WWW.FACTHOUND.COM.
JUST TYPE IN THE BOOK ID: 9781434221520 AND YOU'RE READY TO GO!